She looked at him calmly. "Will you marry me?" she asked.

"You're rich," he told her.

"Is there something wrong with that?"

He cleared his throat. "Look, nobody could ever say I'd let a woman keep me."

"Come off it," she told him.

"I'd have to have something in my own name. Say, fifty thousand."

"Five," she said. "Full wardrobe, a car, plus five."

This was the beginning—of one of the strangest, most *amoral* unions ever made—an unnatural alliance spawned of the darkest, twisted urgings of man and woman . . .

THE BEDSIDE CORPSE

Complete and Unabridged

The Bedside Corpse

(Original Title: *The Gray Eyes*)

Stuart Friedman

WILDSIDE PRESS

The Bedside Corpse
(The Gray Eyes)

Published by Wildside Press LLC
www.wildsidepress.com

For My Wife,
Jeanette Arnold Friedman

PART ONE

CHAPTER I

ONCE, AT A RESTAURANT PARTY, NORA Emlaine excused herself graciously and went to the ladies' lounge. Her husband had noticed her looking peevishly at her hands and, accustomed to her overfastidiousness, had assumed that, even in the middle of the meal, she was going to wash. When she returned, fur coat slung about her shoulders, stares and titters followed her. He saw she was barefooted. Swiftly his eyes sought hers. But she was not seeing him. Her eyes had the dogged and pleading look of a child who knew she would be punished and wanted it not to be so. Before he could react further she settled herself into her chair, letting her coat slide casually from her shoulders onto the chairback. She was naked.

It was shortly after that, that she began to refer to herself as a widow. She would laugh, a funny little girl's laugh, and look at her husband reprovingly, as though to say he mustn't tease, when he would ask if she thought he wasn't there.

Of course he was there. But he was dead.

Nora tried to remain patient with him. She was aware that he was stupid and weak. But he persisted in touching her, or he might place an unexpected kiss on her ear or neck from behind and she would have to go at once to wash. Often in the middle of the night she would wake in horror to his touch and hear him begging like a craven animal to come back to life. He was too obtuse to understand that he had outworn her tolerance. She supposed she might have let herself be obvious and vulgar and stated explicitly that she found him no more acceptable in death than during his life. But it

9

would have been a useless waste of herself. She was surely not interested in anyone who lacked perception to such a degree that he needed words to explain a situation.

When she first went to Freelands Sanitarium she was extremely docile. She was pleased with its polite, hushed atmosphere, the reserved deference of the others. She was uncommunicative, yet responsive, as though passively absorbing the fine, rolling grounds, the landscaped gardens and terraces, the cloistered buildings, the strange people and conditions. Since she was young and very pretty, with rich reddish-brown curly hair, a pale, small oval face, soft, long-lashed violet eyes and a dulcet little-girl voice, attendants and patients alike were charmed by Nora.

She was gracefully slender, and while not petite, she had an air of hesitancy and uncertainty that made her seem frail. The others recognized a helplessness that they knew so well within themselves, and automatically sought to protect it with what amounted to a sort of yearning and frightened instinct of self preservation. On morning walks, in the game rooms and handicraft shops, in the softlighted, spacious, and comfortably appointed evening lounge, groups clustered about her as though to guard a precious, tender core. They were eager to teach, to encourage, to console . . . and to confide. Nora at first responded warmly to their recognition that she was one to be treasured. She had long known it. Only others had doubted, forced her to test the depth of their regard, the strength of her position.

These sought approval, and offered up their skills and talents. An elderly composer set to work on a symphony and suffered a relapse; a young man wrote poems; a fat, homely, middle-aged woman who had not spoken one word in years nor offered anything to anyone began to send crochet work, watching from a distance as the attendant delivered it, then turning abruptly so that she might not accept so much as a smile or glance in return.

One man told Nora that he knew who she was, that he prayed before her shrine and privately underwent the sacred punishments she inflicted. There was, however, something about his eyes that frightened while it attracted her, so that she kept him at a distance. But she kept him, managing a smile of invitation and understanding that was both a bridge and a barrier. He never came near. Which was right.

There was one unpleasant incident. A feud, climaxing in a wild screeching, clawing, slapping, hair-pulling fight, developed between two women over Nora. She was hurt, but not surprised when the attendants seemed to blame her. She had done nothing. But she realized that this was their way of acknowledging her strength.

As Nora became more certain of her position, the savor went out of it. She had charm, she knew; beauty, she knew. And she had been nice to them. She became less inclined to bestow smiles. She received attentions and courtesies coolly, her violet eyes unresponsive. The inhabitants of this domain were abject; they had accorded her dominance. Now she rewarded them with derision and a soft-voiced scorn. She began to give orders to see who would take them. She appointed servants and set tasks for them. She would break into a card game, require one of the players to leave and rub her head or comb her hair, or increasingly, to brush her shoes or stroke her feet.

Gradually this drove many of them away and, though she resented the defections bitterly, she soon lost interest in these. When, one after another, most had withdrawn, as she had known they would, there were still the two women who had fought over her. They vied to serve her and she pitted them against one another, so that they sought to circumvent the attendants with every wile for the privilege of her boundless contempt. At first Nora had found it interesting to test the limit to which she could degrade them; but there was no limit,

11

no shame. They were dogs, and when they had the chance they licked her feet, literally. She despised them both, but she couldn't quite bring herself to have them officially constrained. She contrived to spirit one or the other of them to her private room almost every day and order the woman to get under the bed, at her feet, while she stood, somehow wildly excited by the physical mastery. Often she would beat the woman savagely on the back with her fists when she crawled out. Or she would pull her hair, hissing an order for absolute silence.

Finally one of the doctors caught her and she and the two women were kept under such constant surveillance there was no chance for these delights to continue.

There was one old woman who constantly whispered behind her hand and Nora hated her on sight. She did not go near the old woman; she didn't know nor care what it was she whispered. The fact of the gray hair had incensed her, and she always walked away hurriedly, face flushing, if the woman gave any indication of coming near.

A few nights after getting caught by the doctor Nora was aware, as she ate dinner, of a hissing whisper from a table behind her. She tried to ignore it. From the phonograph there came a sonorous, undulating flowline of Debussy and it was peaceful there in the high-ceilinged, draped room set with small, intimate tables. The patients ate quietly, withdrawn and calm. Only the smallest of sounds, the tinkle of a fork, a subdued murmur were audible under the music. Nora felt a comfortable day-end tiredness and the food, which she ate slowly and thoroughly, savoring every morsel, was good.

She heard the behind-the-hand whispering again, an ugly sound from a hated face, and tried to shut it out.

She would love the music; it gave her a sweet, languorous feeling of pleasant aloneness, and she paused between bites, listening distantly, her body unconsciously, almost imperceptibly swaying. She felt happily that she was suspended in space and that she was moving weightless and pliant on the waves of sound.

The hissing whisper began again. Nora rose, turned, walked in her characteristic effortlessly graceful way. She paused behind the old woman's chair, and bending as though to retrieve some trifle she grasped the chair legs, yanked them and spilled the woman to the floor. Without visible haste, her face devoid of hostility she caught two fistfuls of gray hair and forced the old woman's face down to her own feet. Attendants rushed her and she leaped away, screeching and flailing and ripping at her clothes. She kicked and struck at one of them as he touched her. She darted wildly between tables, lithe and mercurial, feinting and dancing out of reach. Waiters, attendants, the doctor-in-charge set out in pursuit. The other patients set up a bedlam, leaping up and milling frenziedly.

She collided with patients, chairs, tables; at last crawled under a table. She'd ripped the whole front of her dress open. She locked her arms around the table legs, screamed as they pried her loose. Then she stood limp and docile until she felt the slight relaxation of the grip on her arms. She suddenly dove forward, butted headlong with her full weight into the stomach of one of them. Recaptured, she struck out with her feet and knees. As she was subdued she screamed steadily, filling her lungs, screaming herself breathless, drawing in air, screaming again, her eyes mashed shut.

They carried her out with lock grips on her ankles and wrists. She twisted and writhed and yanked, thrusting her arms and legs, doubling herself, arching her back rigidly, screaming, screaming incessantly to the end of her breath. In the physiotherapy room they gagged and trussed her and doused her with water and slapped and pommeled her and wrenched her arms so badly she could barely lift them for days.

13

The first time they allowed her back in the dining room she started to undress. She tried at every meal. When she was sent to her room she refused to leave again for any reason and had to be dragged out, clawing and kicking and cursing. At last they allowed her to stay in the room all the time.

She was happy alone, painting. A nurse or a doctor would oblige when she requested a theme. She would thank them elaborately for telling her what to paint, then set to work, smiling, enrapt, painting something else.

She alone knew about The Gray Eyes. It was under their direction that she would paint. She would work steadily, absorbed until she finished a canvas to their satisfaction, whether it took an hour or a week. Finished, she would take a small brush, and with green paint carefully obliterate the picture, stroking thin, waving lines across the canvas, line after narrow line from top to bottom, until in the end, each work was a solid expanse of green.

There were times when The Gray Eyes wanted her to paint something quite distasteful to her, and then she might delay sullenly or angrily daub and spatter paint on blankets, pillow and bedposts. But in the end she would yield, smiling a little guiltily.

She was supposed to consult weekly with the doctor-proprietor of Freelands, but during this period she would not go to his office. If coerced into going, she simply refused to speak. He was a man. He came to her. She would watch his eyes slink down to her nylon-sheathed ankles and try to crawl between her knees into the shadows under her skirt. She would talk to him with words, amused with his notion that he was guiding and controlling the consultation.

It was fun to talk along with her mouth, saying nothing as she slyly moved him like a puppet. She would let her hand lie as though unaware, provocatively limp in the hollow between her thighs. Then she would brush her fingers languorously over the skirt to out-

14

line her legs more clearly and lift one leg, extending her foot casually as she talked, turning it as though aimlessly exercising her ankle. As he watched she would stop speaking abruptly, trapping his gaze there, off-limits. She would remain obdurately silent until he was forced to look at her in tacit confession, and her smile would scoff as she made her lips sweetly shape a murmured "No."

Her husband came to visit her weekly at this time but after each visit Nora would stay in bed, refusing to wash, resisting every effort by the attendants to wash her. If they succeeded she rolled naked on the floor, scouring dirt into her palms and smearing her face. She would not use either the toilet or bedpan in the days following his visit. She would soil herself in the bed and lie giggling, defiant and triumphant. The orgies of dirt were inevitably followed by equally exaggerated cleaning and scrubbing. Then again, the painting, and the painstaking obliteration of the work with green wavy lines.

At the request of the doctor, her husband stopped his weekly visits. When they were resumed, she was docile, sweetly responsive to him and to the attendants. She had no aftermaths of filthifying herself. The Gray Eyes had said she must leave Freelands. The Gray Eyes, who had watched her since shortly after her marriage, unblinking, every moment of every day and night, and who heard and understood the unspoken, and who advised and scolded and guided, knowing all things, always, and to whom she was always pure and naked and beautiful, had said that she must leave Freelands. So she was very, very good. Her improvement was soon noticeable. She really did feel better, sweeter. But, more important than that, she had a plan and a duty.

She made an "Amends" list, and to each of those in the sanitarium she had hurt she offered an abject apology.

"I have been sick," she said, "and very unpleasant, I

15

am sure. I'm sorry." She seemed again to be the girl they had cherished in the beginning.

Deep within her she knew that it was they who had offended her, each of them. An offense to Nora was to yield to her, to surrender and serve, to show weakness. Nora did not forget, nor forgive. An offense registered indelibly and could never be obliterated. It stood, indestructible in her mind, concealed and dim sometimes as a painting in a gallery at night. But it could no more be destroyed than could a work of art or of any perfection. Existing once, the offense existed forever. Only The Gray Eyes could have ordered her to make amends.

She was powerless before The Gray Eyes, obedient. For they, and no one else knew her; could not be deceived, outwitted, defeated in any way. She might whisper some lie, in secret, testing. The Gray Eyes were never fooled. Her defeat with them would make her smile with pleasure and feel guarded and secure. Because they saw her always naked and beautiful, and they loved her, but they loved without surrender and they could not be charmed into prideless stupidity and they could not be weaker than she, but stronger, than she, stronger and wiser than all the world and they could not be weaker than flesh nor contemptible and craven.

Always watching, unblinking, seeing her, and her alone, The Gray Eyes approved as she and her husband and the head of the sanitarium had the final consultation.

The two men seemed elated, now and then casting covert glances of pride and triumph at each other because she talked so lucidly, even wittily, of all the matters of a world that once had interested her. As if they were responsible. She had read omnivorously for a week in papers and magazines, knowing the great store set by commonplace minds on commonplaces. She cast her eyes down and with a laughing, embarrassed voice, repented for wantonly exposing her body.

Lowering her tone, sitting with bowed shoulders and watching her hands, she began to speak of her odd, former notion that Mr. Emlaine had been dead. She stopped her breath in catches sometimes in the middle of words and knew that she looked fraily lovely and altogether wretched with remorse.

Of course they would have had to release her anyway. She had not after all been really committed. But she knew, exultantly, that guided by The Gray Eyes she had forced them to see her as better, had forced them to see things her way, do what she wanted. As she felt her husband's arm around her shoulders and his hand gripping her arm supportively, and heard his voice, low and huskily near tears, she bit her inner cheek to keep from laughing. He was the same, the same.

Riding comfortably relaxed on the trip home to New York, letting the gentle motion of the heavy car lull her, she watched the landscape of fields and woods and occasional houses. The view didn't interest her. It was the only alternative to looking at the dull back of the chauffeur's head or at her husband.

She was well now. Once she had done indiscreet things and had had foolish imaginings. It was madness to imagine a man dead when the rest of the world was incapable of imagining it. She sighed.

She would not be mad if she imagined him dead and he really was. A smile flickered, curving her cheek momentarily, and she heard him ask delightedly what was going on in that adorable little head.

The Gray Eyes knew.

CHAPTER II

NORA WANDERED INTO THE BATHROOM, tested the water, wandered back, listened vaguely to the low sound of the radio, drifting quietly. She lighted a cigarette, her mind worrying the shattering discovery.

The Gray Eyes had a body!

He wore clothes like all other men. Gray suit, hat, topcoat, black shoes, like other men. Once he'd taken off his hat and he had the sort of hair all men had, medium dark and parted on the side.

Most incredible, he had a name. "Ed." The girl with him had said, "Ed." "What's a Tiglon, Ed? . . . Ed, you are not supposed to smoke here inside the lion house . . . Ed, they give me the shivers the way they pace, the way they look at you . . ."

Nora had wanted to say, "You have a name, too."

Time and again, first by the seal pond, later at the fence waching the camels, later in the house of the big cats she had wanted to say: "You have a name, too." When he had tried to see what she was drawing, she had hastily written in big block letters across the lioness' head she was sketching, "I don't like that name."

She would never have chosen such a name for him.

But whatever the name was, the oddest part was that the girl with him—a cheap, giddy little person in bargain-basement leopard stencilled mouton and a face, fluffed around as it was with taffy hair and a nose pink with cold, far more like a rabbit's than a leopard's—called him by that dull name as though he had always had it. She had chattered to him as though knowing him, accepted him as though he had always been, and thought there was nothing strange in his having a

18

name and a body and clothes like other men, as though he had always had those things.

All afternoon, all evening, half the sleepless night, Nora had thought about that. She had got up at last, tuned in an all-night radio program, set the water running in the tub. Now she stood before her dresser and looked thoughtfully at her left hand, then slipped off the engagement and wedding diamonds, put them in her jewel box. It was only right. Her husband was dead. His body had been removed to the funeral home. He had been buried weeks ago.

The police had come, the police had gone. The polite and believing pink-faced inspector, the detectives and uniformed policemen had all called it suicide. The reporters, the men at the funeral home, business associates and friends, Mr. Emlaine's attorney, her friends, her doctor were all believing. They had been gentle with her, fearing that this new tragedy coming so fast upon her trouble might disturb her. They had hovered over her protectingly.

By his own hands he had died; hanged himself in this very bathroom.

How believing!

The Gray Eyes knew.

And—disturbingly—The Gray Eyes had a body.

In the weeks of widowhood Nora had been happy. She had been alone, except for the servants. Now and then a friend had phoned or come. They sometimes tried to insert themselves in her life; sometimes tried to whine "comfort" to her for her "bereavement." ". . . so terrible for you, Nora, on Christmas day too . . . but you must try to live, dear, not shut yourself away . . . he wouldn't have wanted that . . ." Then always, later, the dear friends would purr and try to pull it out of her: ". . . but why did he *do* it, dear? . . . what happened that night, dear? . . ." To one of them, Nora had said, lowering her voice, bending forward: "Wipe the spit off your chin—you're drooling, darling." Their lascivious

19

minds always came back to the tantalizing notion that Mr. Emlaine in a fit of madness and thwarted craving for her beautiful body, had trod into the bathroom and jumped into a noose. A passionate man. That's what he'd liked them to think. He had confided to an intimate core of friends, and the notion had become a secret known to everyone, that his was an insatiable passion, and she, some aloof exquisite idol who must be courted anew each time she was sought.

It was untrue. She had never withheld herself from him. She had scorned such petty devices. A wife wasn't some unattainable idol. A wife had duties. Nora had fulfilled hers. When he won her, he always knew he had won nothing. She had allowed him to know that, wordless, unmoved. His piddling little gallantries, his fevered surges of passionate love-making were accepted, passively.

Nora had been quite alone since Christmas, and never happier. Often the chauffeur would drive her for a few hours—wherever he chose. Usually she spent her afternoons walking, sketching in Central Park, or sitting on a bench. She had sketched in the zoo a few times. She liked the big cats. Sometimes she thought of going to the beach to watch the ocean, but the notion wasn't very pleasant, and when the chauffeur would choose such a route she would look away or doze. The Gray Eyes had scarcely ever been near.

But now!

Now! She went back to the tub, shut off the water. Unblinking gray eyes, watching, unblinking.

"Ed." Why had he chosen such a name? And that body. She was a little puzzled that he had done so much on his own accord. From all she could see he had chosen a good enough body—but how had he presumed to do it? And why? Though the body seemed all right, it was far from the perfection she would have chosen. He was tall, but not tall enough. He looked strong, but his chest set too near his hips; she'd have

20

liked a long-waisted body for him. What his musculature was could only be guessed . . . fair, she gauged. Not godlike though, she thought, a touch peevishly.

Well, there was nothing to be done now. Ed was her own creation, and if he'd muffed it on the choice of a body she had only herself to blame. She had been careless. The late Mr. Emlaine had said she had a large streak of carelessness in her. She laughed aloud, remembering, and thought he had had a rather more serious sort of carelessness about him or he would still have been flesh instead of ashes. It was as nourishing as a good meal to have the final laugh. But after it she pressed the back of her hands against her lips and looked around uncertainly, like a child fearful of being caught at a forbidden pleasure.

Ed! Why, oh why in hell hadn't she been more careful in creating him? In fact, all she had ever attended to were his eyes. Just the eyes, unblinking gray eyes. They had been all she'd ever attended to through all the years. Just eyes, watching, unblinking gray eyes. Detached. They might, in fact, even have been women's eyes. Of course she had known they were men's eyes. Now it was done. He existed. She had dreamed him into reality, and he WAS. The forehead was high and wide, which was good. Yes, quite good. His lower face was— well—there was something a little wrong there. The way it tapered down from the cheekbones, narrowing to the chin, giving him that rather wise animal look! It was like a muzzle, she decided, the tapering muzzle of a wise animal.

She should really have dreamed him in detail and fully from hair to feet and given him the face and the bodily structure which would have fulfilled her vague ideal of male perfection. It irked her. Someone had said, someone famous, that there were no details in a work of art. No fragment could be unimportant to an artist. Each bit had equal value to the real artist; nothing was a trifle, nothing should be sloughed over. But it was untrue! She

21

was an artist. The petty daubers with paint and the tinklers with sound worked with trifling, restricted little impressions which required painstaking tedious touches. The matters which she dealt with had never actually been small enough for any formal setting. Others had never understood the vastness of her concepts, and so they had seemed vague.

Thinking of Ed, she jabbed at the bell with an angry forefinger, several times, calling the servant. Perhaps Ed was NOT her creation . . . if only she could seriously doubt him. She couldn't. The eyes. The unblinking gray eyes . . . they had been gone, gone without her consciously willing it. Gone all these weeks. She understood vaguely why. The deep—deep—deep mind in her, the mind she had held inviolate, closed off, personal, sacred from the spidery sneakings of the psychoanalyst who, before she went to Freelands, had tried to probe it—that deep-artist mind had all the while been at work. Without her even realizing it, it had worked to produce Ed. But he was flawed.

Or was he? Wasn't he really perfect? Hadn't she created better than even she yet knew; didn't he probably fulfill in detail what had only been her vague ideal of perfection?

The servant, Mrs. Trent, was long in coming. When she did appear Nora looked briefly at her hateful face, sleepily sour, summoned her into the bathroom and got in the tub. She bathed leisurely, ignoring her.

The Gray Eyes had never blinked because they could not risk shutting her out of view, because they existed only because she created them, and they were incapable of seeing anything but her. If they blinked and lost her for even the fraction of a second they died. To them, she existed as though detached, their creator existing detached in space. They couldn't see the walls behind her, nor the floor she trod, nor the chair she sat in. Not even, of course, the clothes she wore. The Gray Eyes saw her always naked and beautiful.

22

If the eyes were his only hold on existence, and if they didn't exist when he was not seeing her—and they were now in a body—she felt confused.

His voice had been smooth and deep, but without any brute-bass undertone. It was clear. The words he spoke had been ordinary. Now that she remembered, it was puzzling that through the years he had not had a voice at all. His words would impress themselves in her hearing, but they hadn't had sound to them.

She stopped thinking about him. She would go to the Central Park Zoo again. He would be there.

CHAPTER III

"THREE BLACK COFFEES," ED CALLED.

Lights, pouring down on the gleaming, perforated metal counter of the cafeteria, glared into his eyes. A woman crowded him, peering, her face thrust out looking at the pastry, commanding the counter man: "What's them? No—them back there over toward this, yeh them, one of them . . . Coffee extra light, two sugars." "Sugar on the table, lady," the counter man lavished patience on her. Ed fingered the rough, chipped rim of his tray. This hangover had begun before he even got drunk, went to bed with him, woke him twenty times in the night with an agony of weakness in his stomach, sent him to the bathroom trying to vomit four useless times; left him lying trembling, dizzy, the overpowering waves of pain coming in long, rhythmic surges into his skull.

He had been exhausted when he got up for the day. He'd forced himself to walk two miles, fast, dragging the cold, dead, morning air into his lungs, trying to burn the poison out of him. He'd drunk three nauseating foamy glasses of seltzer, and they set now in an icy lump in his stomach. There was a fine sweat over his body, and his leg muscles throbbed after the fast walking, but his head was worse. He thought if he bent over he'd spill the icy lump of seltzer all over the place . . . he could feel it surge a little, as if it were coming up, and he swallowed quickly several times, trying to hold on. The coffees were coming across the counter. He put his check on the counter, lifted the cups carefully one after another onto the tray as the counter man punched and crimped the check, pushing it at him, his face ignoring him.

Ed carried the tray, sloshing the coffee, found an empty table full of dirty dishes beside the broad plate glass windows in front. He let himself down heavily on a chair, still in overcoat and hat, left the coffee on the tray. He lifted one cup. He took a sip, half-scalding his upper lip, set the cup down with a clank, tipping and spilling a quarter of it.

He sat staring sightlessly ahead of him and tried to breathe evenly and slowly, wanting to throw the cups and the tray, wanting to upset the table, wanting to smash a chair through the plate glass. He opened his mouth and drew in a breath, letting it circulate coldly on his palate and tongue. There was ground glass through him . . . he detested . . . detested, nothing in particular, everything . . . himself, his life, the cheap tawdriness of his life. A dream of changing it all tried to stir. But he had not the strength to maintain it.

He hunched over, lifted a cup in both hands, closed his eyes and drank it slowly, letting it roll hot and gagging over his tongue and down his throat. He lighted a cigarette; the smoke was tasteless, thin and flat. For a while he sat inert and very still, easing his breath in and out slowly, trying to smooth out the waves of pain in his head for a little while at least.

He sat looking at the other coffees, trying to decide if he could take them. The taste of the first hung on, bitter and stale as from old grounds. A bus boy came and began clearing the table, clattering dishes into one another, scraping food remnants off with sharp, choppy sounds, piling plates with a careless crash, then smearing a garbagey smelling film over the table with a dirty wet rag. A sweep of nausea ran the length of Ed's body and dull anger set his heart pumping heavily. His eyes bleared with the intensity of pain in his head. His right arm hung straight down along his side to the chair rung, and he was aware that what was left of his cigarette was in that hand. He needed a drag, and he didn't want to move; he thought of stirring, tensing muscles to get the arm up made him almost cringe. His arm felt stiff as a log, and heavy; he sat trying to decide if he could get his hand up to his face. His palms were both dry, and the skin felt thick and leathery. The smoke came sifting up hotly along his fingers, getting up his sleeve. Under his clothes he felt damp and a little chilly. He didn't think he wanted to break or smash anything anymore. He didn't want to do anything but just sit, because he didn't see how he could ever get up the energy to move. He looked blearily at the tray and cups wishing they were on the other side of the table so he could lie forward and rest a little bit. Somewhere blurrily underneath was the faint urgency to stir himself. But he couldn't think of any reason to stir . . . he thought if he got over to the office and got seated maybe he could rest a little there. It was a long way back home. He looked out of the corner of his eyes at the gray-ugly cold street and shivered. It was warm here. He felt the cigarette fall on the floor out of his slack fingers and his chin sank down toward his chest.

Someone was clanking something, and he opened his eyes, put out his hand falteringly toward the tray being removed.

"'M dring coffee . . . dringing it, now . . . leave coffee . . ."

He put his hand out and curled a forefinger in the handle, and looked at it, felt his eyes closing in spite of him. . . . He'd rouse every few seconds and curl his finger tighter in the cup handle . . . the sounds in the cafeteria swam, blurred and comforting, in and out of his consciousness; he could feel his lips thickening with a crust and now and then self-consciously shut his mouth, looked up guiltily, his eyes open, but asleep tried to remember to breathe through his nose. . . . But the heavy, heavy, good heavy languor settled down on him. . . . He woke with a sharp start as someone bumped his chair, and his hand automatically lifted, spilling coffee.

He roused himself dully, straightened, his brows bunching. He picked up the coffee, drank it cold. The pain in his head was much less severe. He got a fresh cigarette, inhaled deeply enough to feel the thick heavy column of smoke in his windpipe. He dragged several times and got to his feet and looked around for his check. It was gone. He groped in his pockets. It was gone. It meant going to the manager, talking, explaining, waiting. . . . He unbuttoned his coat and looked in his jacket. He felt in his pants pockets. He had to get out of here. The place was stifling him. He didn't want to have to wait and explain, to argue, to wait. He had to get out of here. He probed under his jacket to his shirt pocket, which was stuck fast together with starch. He dug against it, trying to get his fingers into it. Part of him knew the check couldn't be there if the pocket was glued fast that way, but it became vital to loosen the pocket. He held his breath, digging clumsily, then gave it up, a hellish weakness coming over him. He felt as if he wanted to cry. He pushed at the tray, searching for the check again. He started through his overcoat pockets, the side pockets, the inside one, the jacket pockets, his pants hip pockets, digging down around the bulky wad of a dirty handkerchief. He looked back on the tray, then picked it up and found the check. The tension fell away from him miraculously.

It was three blocks down Third Avenue, half a block west to the dingy, beat-up tenement converted into mangy offices. He climbed slowly to the third floor,

26

went to the end of the unlighted short hall, opened the unmarked door into the "boiler room" of 5-A Ad Agency.

It was the usual smoky, noisy bedlam inside. Ed found an empty hook among the hats and overcoats hanging along the side wall. He acknowledged the hand waves, the greeting nods, and settled into his chair among them at the long littered table. A dozen men, ranged along both sides of the table, sat smoking, shuffling through clutters of paper, scribbling, dialing phones and pouring out streams of high-pressure oil into those phones. There was a dirty window at one end of the room, opened a few inches top and bottom, giving a view of a crumbling red brick wall two feet away. On one side of the window were a pair of mud-colored, chip-paint three-section bath screens arranged to form the manager's private office. On the other side of the window a sharp faced blonde sat plunking a battered old typewriter set beside a gooseneck lamp and wire baskets on a kitchen table. The manager was out, as usual. This was where the work was done, but 5-A Ad Agency maintained an uptown office.

Frowning against the cone light two feet above the tabletop in front of him Ed opened his drawer, took out pencils, scratch pads, copy pads, order book, a typed list of firm names filling several stapled sheets. Beside the typed names were his own penciled notations, numerals of 5–10–25, or question marks; "Call Fri. 10:30"; "See lead . . .," "Tap—good ten only, tho——," "Call again —mention Fox Ad," "Offer exclusive if take back cover ——." He was half through the list. Beside most of the finished calls was the tiny, barely decipherable note: "NG." Others showed large "Sold—10 . . . sold 10 . . . sold 10 . . . sold 5–5–5–5–5–SOLD $50." That last had been only yesterday. Fifty bucks, half a page ad. And paid on the barrelhead. Twenty bucks commission. He still had three dollars and some change.

He unbuttoned his jacket, loosened his tie, lighted a smoke, scooted his chair nearer the table. Had to get to work. He looked down to the end of the table at the alarm clock: 10:40. Damned near noon. Maybe if he held off and started fresh after lunch . . . Well, he'd knocked off yesterday afternoon after he got that twenty bucks so fast. What he had to do was keep hitting. Stack up some money, settle down. Get something in the bank, sack it up . . . and get married.

He set his cigarette in a groove gouged and burned into the thick dark wood of the scarred old table, penciled in the date on the top printed white order blank. He lifted the corners carefully, making sure the writing came through the carbons to the pink duplicate and green triplicate. He straightened the slips of carbon paper, realigned his chair, inspected the clean top sheet of his copy pad, saw it was faintly indented from yesterday's doodling on a sheet above. He tore and wadded the marred sheet, scooted the phone a little to his left, then to the right, picked up his cigarette for a drag, glanced down at the alarm clock.

He drew a neat box on his copy pad, and looking at the first uncrossed-out name on his typed list wrote the firm name in the box, noted wryly the penciled $5. Two big bucks commission. Sometime. The five-buck buyers didn't pay on the barrelhead.

Ed tried to remember if he'd said anything personal to Edna yesterday. Anything about marriage. Not in the afternoon, he hadn't. She had sure been tickled with the surprise date. That had been some gag, telegraphing her office that her old man was sick and getting her off work. They'd gone uptown to Central Park and just drifted around, going to the zoo there, not drinking anything at all. Ed and Edna. She liked to make something out of that. A nice kid, but maybe it had been a damnfool trick going to that trouble with the telegram, maybe making her think she meant more than she did to him. She was cute, too, very cute . . . but . . . well, it was a lousy way to think about her that she'd seemed maybe a little coarse. Cheap clothes, and she chattered too

28

much. Nice, she'd make a good wife, but not class. That redhead with the violet eyes drawing the lions there in the zoo . . . she'd been all cream, and under-glass soft, and that beaver coat wasn't imitation—nothing imitation about that, she was perfect . . . beautiful, beautiful . . . made you ache to think about her. It was lousy putting Edna up against a dame like that, it was lousy . . . but she'd been giving him the eye, he knew that much. God, if he'd been alone! Soft, creamy, perfumed . . . nothing cheap or coarse there . . . brought up in a hothouse . . . none of that gritty, loud mouth, cheap, harsh . . .

Eight to eleven. The blonde was getting up and in-to her coat . . . coffee time. He dug automatically in his pocket for change, withdrew his hand empty. He didn't think he'd stick around. He watched absently as the blonde lingered by Paul Chessly, the ex-actor—the dude, the smooth hijacker. Ex-actor, always mouth-ing about the walk-on he'd refused *last* week, or the solid piece he was considering *now,* or the fix he was going to be in *next* week trying to choose between two parts. He always seemed to have chosen the one in between the two. He did all right on the phone without ever seeming to strain himself. He seemed to have some good, steady taps, and now and then he'd leave off cleaning his fingernails, dial a number, and lie back in his chair and come up wearily after a time and write out an order in a desultory way as if on the verge of collapse from boredom. None of the gang liked Paul Chessly. He was a little too smooth, and most of them figured he had a sharper angle than the suave threats stand-ard with 5-A.

An ex-actor, an ex-preacher, ex-pug, ex-detective, ex-bookkeeper, ex-tout, even an ex-advertising man. Every-body in 5-A was ex-something. They were all expert blackmailers, but it was petty larceny. The suspicion that Paul Chessly's was bigger league made him en-vied, but not condemned.

It was the hell of hangovers, Ed thought. It made things too clear. Not worse than they were, but *what* they were. Shabby and lousy. His fifty buck deal yesterday was pocketpicking, and he knew it. Maybe he'd have felt better about it if the money hadn't gone down the drain, but it had. It always did . . . himself with it, getting scummier and trickier and sharper all the time. Someday, sometime, he'd latch on the real thing. But then he cursed, knowing it wasn't true.

He'd put out the "amateur" spiel, stumbled over his tongue, got the guy to pretend he was selling himself. Ed had told the sucker that he was a member of the lodge which was publishing the annual souvenir booklet, that he was giving his time free, that he was phoning from a list made out by the lodge president (Ed had called him by his front name) and the lodge president had marked down $50 beside the name. Then Ed had ingratiatingly laughed and said he considered that a mighty fine amount, and paused, letting the sucker remember that the lodge president in question happened to be a customer who spent thousands with the sucker's firm. It was true that the lodge people had provided them with lists of firms, and that 5-A was sometimes able to get close co-operation from the organization theoretically publishing the booket as to the amounts spent by members with various businesses. Lots of the ads were simple donations, good will, and ran anonymously as "Compliments of a Friend."

Paul Chessly was getting up and into his coat; Ed decided to knock off too. No percentage in sitting around killing off possibles. They weren't that easy come by. He caught a bus and went to his room and fell into a dead sleep.

He had the damnedest thought when he woke in the middle of the afternoon.

"I'm the only one that's not an ex-something."

Oh, he'd worked before landing in this scummy racket. He'd run errands, clerked, sold newspapers and subscriptions, jerked sodas, washed dishes. Nothing that he could be an ex of though. Ex-dishwasher, he tried aloud and laughed at himself.

And suddenly he felt pretty good, knowing there was nowhere to go but up. He thought of the woman and pushed the thought out of his head. He thought instead of Edna and decided to phone her. No hurry though . . . It should wait a day. . . . It should wait, in fact. He remembered he'd got maudlin. There wasn't any real question about whether he'd said anything personal. The only question was how tight had she been . . . not enough gone to forget. . . . Hell, what had he told her? The whole scummy works: ". . . You'd think it was a line if I told you something, Edna. . . ."

"No I wouldn't, Ed."

Jeez, he'd felt good. Sitting there snug as hell in the booth with her, warm as hell inside, not drinking much, just enough—always just enough, always with the next drink waiting to make him feel a little better. Sort of mellow, sort of feeling her admiration, her tenderness.

"Sure, you'd think it was a line."

"Ed, I wouldn't, honest, not anything you told me. Some fellas I would. Most fellas I would. . . ."

"I'm just like all the rest." Then he'd downed the drink. "Maybe worse, I dunno. With a girl like you I feel like I'd like to be better than that . . . I dunno . . . I dunno, maybe I'm drunk. . . ." She'd snuggled a little closer till he could feel her hip and leg against his, her shoulder against his arm, her face watching his profile.

"Yeah, just drunk. It's the real me, the drunk . . . no guts. . . ." He'd sighed and waited for a denial and had to repeat "No guts" before he got it. "No . . . no . . . no . . . if there was anything real about me I could say all these things to you. When I'd catch myself dreaming about you, how I want you, how sometimes your face is there—when I'd catch myself I'd come and tell you . . . it'd give you a good laugh . . .?"

31

"Oh . . . Ed."

She'd put her hand in his. It had felt good, and he'd pressed it. "It's what happened this afternoon," he told her. "I had to be with you . . . that crazy telegram. . . ."

"It wasn't crazy."

"Then I didn't have the guts to tell you," he said. "That's the real me."

He'd kissed her right there in the booth. Sloppy, slobbery . . . half-knowing how maudlin he'd got. ". . . protective . . . p'tective . . . tective . . . ma'me feel p'tective . . . Enna, want you, want you always, always wannit EdnEnna . . . EdnEnna . . ."

Remembering, he grinned at himself, but it was sour. It was a good line, better than his phone spiel. He'd kept thinking about the under-glass creamy redhead who'd given him the eye at the Central Park Zoo. Most of the evening he'd thought about her while he was pouring the whisky in and the line out to Edna. He'd stare at his drink and cigarette while he talked, and imagine it wasn't Edna's body wilted against him, not her slightly stubby hand entwined in his. He'd imagined it wasn't Edna listening to the one story he never told anybody unless he was mawkish drunk.

He remembered he'd gone silent for a little while and disengaged her hand and opened his own right hand palm up on the table, showing the white scar that ran diagonally from the outer heel to the base of his forefinger. She had exclaimed when he put the ember of his cigarette close to the scar as if he was going to burn himself. She hadn't even known he had that scar. He told her about it. It had yanked them both almost sober.

It had happened when he was ten, in the little Western town where he'd been born. His father had got shot in the chest. They'd brought him home and it had taken hours for him to die, and Ed had been with him, and the old man talked and cried with the pain and tried to tell Ed how it felt. Like a poker through his chest, like a hot poker through his chest, white hot, not just red hot, and the old man had talked and cried and talked there in the bedroom alone with Ed and tried to describe the pain and asked Ed to get a bucket of water and pour it in the hole, though it was just agonized talking, and it couldn't be done. Just him and the old man there in the bedroom.

Ed's mother had stayed out, stayed out till very near the end; and Ed had been the one to hear it all, to listen to the old man in his pain begging for forgiveness. Ed remembered going crying, pleading to his mother and how it hadn't done any good and how she wouldn't come. Then at the last, when the old man was about to go for good, forever, she'd finally come.

The old man had been handsome and it had been another man's wife that caused it, and it was called justifiable, but he could never forget that agony and the way the old man had begged for his wife to come, and described the pain, like fire in him, like fire burning in the flesh like a white-hot poker in there, run through his chest, and sometimes taking Ed's hand and almost mashing it without knowing it as the pain would come in an awful spasm . . . and the terrible shining eyes looking at him, and the shuddering way he breathed and told him: "Get her, Eddie, get her to come . . . get her to come . . . I can't stand it no more . . . she can't leave me die and not come. . . ."

The day after his father's funeral Ed had heated a poker in a bellows till it was white hot and looked at it and clenched his teeh and kept looking at it and, being yellow, heating it some more, and crying, and taking it out white hot and looking at it. And then he grabbed the poker in his right fist.

Edna had sat up rigidly away from him, shivering, and instantly he regretted telling her. He'd laughed. He'd lighted a cigarette, blown the ember to a sharp pale orange, touched it to the scar. She'd grabbed his hands, shrieking, and a wave like the shudder from scalding water had raced over his skin from the soles of his feet

33

to his scalp. A waiter had come, frowning, and he'd ordered a double whisky for himself.

He'd kept drinking it and let his tongue slur, trying to feel that he was mellow drunk. But he'd felt gritty and edgy and ashamed. Something he couldn't explain . . . he'd kept feeling more and more lonely with Edna long after she had seemed to forget the story. Lonely as hell. And the whisky smelled bad and tasted bad, and he kept thinking he hadn't eaten since noon; though he'd fed Edna he had wanted his drinks undiluted with food. He'd really begun to feel tender about Edna after he told her that yarn—it was a true yarn—because something always happened after he got drunk and told it. He stopped seeing a girl then. Through the evening he'd kept thinking that it was his late date with her, and it made him lonely and more tender to her.

Before telling her about the poker incident he'd enjoyed half-pretending she wasn't Edna but the girl at the zoo. But afterward, when he found himself thinking of her instead of Edna, it angered him, made him feel he was really a heel because Edna was warmed up to him like she'd never been. He kept trying to sell himself on the idea he meant all he said . . . maybe he even said he loved her. Jeez, he hoped not . . . but he had . . . sure, he knew it.

He ought to phone her, he knew, as he went outside. It was nearly three in the afternoon. He walked over to the subway, rode uptown. He walked into the park toward the zoo. He looked around for a phone . . . there would be one in the cafeteria. He'd promised to phone Edna. He ambled along the edge of the seal pond . . . his glance darted seeing a woman in a beaver coat . . . a pouty-faced little brunette. He edged around a baby carriage . . . looked toward the lion house . . . SHE was there, standing looking in his direction. He started, his heart beginning to pound. He went toward her as she turned casually, went inside, casting a glance over her shoulder. Inviting?

34

When he went inside she was getting a sketch pad out of a zippered case. He strolled, looking at the animals, passed her, almost close enough to brush her coat. A scent of perfume hovered around her. He walked to the end of the passage. He stood at the rail looking in at a big cat pacing nervously from one side of the cage to the other, turning in a whip motion, never taking its eyes from him. Pacing silent, the steel-powered shoulder muscles rippling under the taut coat. He scarcely saw, was only aware of the silent movement, aware that she stood paces down, sketching before another cage. He could feel a mounting tension in himself; his throat was tight with suppressed excitement. He strolled slowly back toward her, trailing his hand along the rail. He kept his teeth clenched, working his jaw muscles nervously, so that they bulged faintly in an even rhythm like a pulse. Then he was standing almost at her elbow. He didn't look at her. He was sharply aware of the scent she wore, a tangy sweetness, a delicate feminine odor sharply contrasting with the smell of the animals which pervaded the place.

His mouth had gone chalk dry. His throat was tight. He could feel the beat of his heart as if the blood throbbed through his windpipe. His coat felt tight over his chest. Somewhere from a cage back of him one of the big cats coughed. Then there was quiet.

He could hear the small padding of the big paws moving quick, nervous, silent on the cage floors. Her pencil moved with swift, short strokes with a faint sluff-sluff; he could see her hand, white and thin, moving gracefully, her wrist curving up out of the rich fur sleeve, her long oval nails painted vivid red, and flashing shimmers and sparks of light as her pencil moved.

The end door opened. Two women and some tiny kids in snowsuits came in and began to run and shout in thin little shrills of joy. He looked toward them, not interested, but her face was in his line of vision. When he turned, she turned. Toward him. Her violet eyes looked at him widely. They stared for seconds, expressionless. He felt his lips parting, and the words locking in the back of his throat. He stood transfixed. Her mouth and cheeks curved in a sudden exquisite smile, then she turned back to her drawing.

"They hate us," he heard her say. "Do you see how they pace and stare, hating us. They are beautiful."

"Yes," he said. "Yes, yes, they're fine looking."

"I hate seeing them confined," she said.

"I guess they don't mind much after awhile. They eat. It's an easy life." Easier than his. But not, he thought with a sudden puzzling flash of enmity as he looked at her, not easier than hers. He let his gaze soften but she turned her eyes away almost as if irritated.

"The good thing is that they never lose their hate," she said as if patiently getting him back on the right track. "Of course if they did that they would die." She was looking at him steadily now. "They would be dead like humans."

"Like humans," Ed laughed uncertainly.

"They are so much finer, so much more beautiful than humans, and the hate stays there in their eyes, no matter how they try and tame them. They can't be tamed. But we spring from monkeys," she said, "instead of cats. Monkeys! You will always find people swarming at the monkey cages."

"That sure is a fact," Ed said. He decided to pay no attention to her words, just her voice; there was something in it that made him ache, like the looks of her. My God, she was beautiful! He had the feeling that he must contribute something, but it was as though he couldn't break into the miracle of her talking to him. He groped for something to say that would make him sound less stupid. But she was talking again, and her pencil moved in abrupt down-slashing strokes filling in a junglelike background for the lion head.

"It's as if the world were backward when puny and prideless little animals can confine a higher species," she

36

said. "I'd like to see them set free sometime when this place is lined with vapid little gawkers."

"I don't think you'd like that," Ed said. "Not really. You think it sounds shocking. I can just imagine your wanting anybody hurt."

She looked at him and giggled. He felt elated. He had *hit*.

"My name is Ed Harlon."

"That sounds like harlot. I don't like it either, but then, of course I'm not sure I don't like it a lot. My late husband said I should have been a whore because I would never be likely to tire out since I never felt anything. I often wondered if a part of me would have made a good one."

He was shocked. Elated, too. She was frank. She liked him. He had fallen into something and come up smelling like a rose!

"Your husband is dead, you say . . ."

"Very definitely this time, as you know, but I wonder, do I want to be a harlot? Do I?"

"Well, no . . . technically, no . . ."

"Technically, yes."

"Sorry, I say no. You're trying to be a shocking little girl again . . . lady, I never met anyone like you. You do have a name?" he asked.

She looked at him in puzzlement. Then, frowning, she turned, and bending, picked up the zippered case, put her drawings away. She didn't turn back to him but went down the passage and out the door. He moved along after her as she turned north along one of the curving, bench-lined walks.

She ignored him as he moved abreast, and continued beside her. She stopped, turned to face him, studying him.

"I'm dreadfully sorry. I don't know you. I thought I did . . ."

"Sure you know me," Ed said, ingratiatingly. "You saw me yesterday."

"I know I did, Mr. Harlon," she said. "But sometimes I—I—imagine. I imagined peculiar things about you . . . but you're just an ordinary flesh and blood man who never set eyes on me till yesterday."

She extended her hand and said: "I'm sorry, Mr. Harlon. Will you just forget this and—and leave me now?"

"Well, of course."

"I talked to you disgracefully . . . but . . . I've been ill. It was kind of you, truly it was . . . I must surely have seemed the veriest tramp. . . ."

"Certainly not, Mrs. . . . uh . . ."

But she didn't give her name. She seemed somehow colder, she seemed to hold herself a little more erect, there was a certain honed look to her face, a hauteur. She seemed really to have come out of a dream and was seeing him disdainfully. He was being dismissed, politely, nicely, but without any mistake. It wasn't coquetry. She'd simply changed her mind about letting him pick her up. He walked away, glancing back hopefully for a few steps until she was out of sight around a turn. He followed her on an impulse. Maybe she'd change her mind again. Walking fast he came in view of her again as she was leaving the path, hurrying across the Fifth Avenue walk to a cab she'd hailed. He watched her settle back, vanish as the cab moved south and cut into the next side street. He strode to the cross street, watched the cab go to Madison Avenue and after a stop at the lights turn north.

He shrugged philosophically, lighted a smoke. He didn't feel philosophical. He felt like hell. To have something like that shoved at you and then for no damned reason yanked away! Damn it. He walked east, headed for a phone booth to call Edna. He changed his mind, and went into the subway. He thought about that . . . her going off in a cab—and him going into the subway.

CHAPTER IV

"You're not looking pleasant," Nora said from the tub. She hated Mrs. Trent, her long face, her gray hair, the sullen gracelessness with which she wore her maid's cap and apron. "You're not looking pleasant at all."

"Ladies' maid ain't my line of work," the woman said, avoiding looking at her.

"Oh," Nora said. "What is your line of work then?" She was rewarded as a swift look of doubt was succeeded by a look of fear as the woman realized how dependent she was on her job with Nora. "You're useless in any other capacity."

"Eight years I worked for the Mr.—bless his soul—and I was satisfactory, none could say different."

"But you see, Nanny—"

"*Please*, Mrs. Emlaine, it's not my name—Nanny!"

"But you see, Nanny," Nora continued, smiling, "I say you are useless in any other capacity. You do as I order, Nanny. You're *old*, Nanny. You are lucky to have any job."

"Well, it's not right waking me every night at three in the morning to help you take a bath."

"Right, Nanny? Do *you* decide on right and wrong?"

"Maybe I don't decide, but I know . . ."

"Oh. You know. But you know, ma'am, don't forget the ma'am."

"Mmmm," Mrs. Trent said, lowering her eyes.

"Let me hear you say it, Nanny."

"I think you're not treating me kind . . . and me an old woman. The Mr. wouldn't have thought well of that."

"Whine, you old thief, I like to hear you whine, but make sure you do as I tell you."

"Thief! . . . why you bitc—" Mrs. Trent paled, gulped

39

away the end of the word. "I'll be leaving such insults. If I can take my pay I'll pack this instant."

"Pay! Pay, Nanny? You are drawn ahead already."

"I am not. . . ."

"*And* you have stolen from me. All of that I shall tell the agencies."

"Well, you'll not . . . you'll not either . . . that you'll not. Why it'd be a sinful lie, and me an old woman with trouble enough to find new work and put out of her home after all these years, me, an old woman . . . are you without mercy, Ma'am?"

"Ma'am . . . that's the way to address me. Now, Nanny, you're learning."

Nora stood up in the tub, extended her hand, wriggling wet fingers. "Come, give me your arm . . . hurry, hurry, Nanny." Nora tossed her head, set her mouth. She snapped her fingers. "You'll have to be more lively, Nanny."

The elderly woman was on the point of tears. She stood staring sickly ahead of her, vaguely seeing Nora Emlaine. Her mouth gaped and she began to blink. She held one hand firmly on the doorknob beside her, and continued to stand, facing the tub. Her ears were aware of the imperious sharp words directed to her; she saw the slim wet hand snapping as though to a dog. She couldn't bear it, she thought.

"I think I'm a bit faint," she said miserably. She snuffed her nose and pulled deeply of the powder- and lotion-scented moist warm air. "I think I need a fresh inhale of air."

"You'll be faint with hunger . . . now listen here, old woman, get the hell over here and do as you're told!"

Mrs. Trent's hand stayed gripped on the doorknob. She felt a small rolling in her stomach and a bitter fluid rose in the back of her mouth. "She can't lie to the agencies about me, she can't keep me from a job, why a worker like me is in great demand . . . why all the while there's a great demand for workers like me . . . respect-

40

able folks. The looks of me isn't the whole tale, no, ma'am, not by far, for I would show by my work how strong I am . . . there's enough ginger in me yet, oh, that's the Lord's truth. Now, sure with some new medicine these terrible tired spells will go . . . yes, it will be a fine adventure to go out searching again, see new people . . ."

Her head began to ache, blindingly; sharp lancets of pain stabbed in her stomach. She was suddenly so tired she wanted to go lie down in her own, small, neatly furnished room in the back of the big apartment. The work had never been too hard; and the other maids and the butler-chauffeur were jolly fun, and Lord, the fine talk and little feasts they'd sometimes have together. She recalled yearningly the little Valentine party when they'd all of them maybe had more than enough to spread the cheer around to each other, and the singing and the great tall tales the butler told in that serious way of his . . . and most of the time Nora Emlaine was in another world. And . . . and then too, Nora herself, bad as she was most of the time, wasn't all bad. Sometimes you could feel right sorry for her, the way she got way off alone some place with her own thoughts, and them not happy ones. Mrs. Trent could remember when Nora had first come to the house, looking like she was scared at the very thought of being married to him . . . and him so gentle.

"I don't want to do anything wrong," she'd said, alone with Mrs. Trent. "I don't want to disturb the way you've always done things."

But of course she had disturbed things. Not quick. But before you noticed it she had things taken over and running her way. She had the Mr. twisted around her finger.

But ever since he'd died the meanness and the spite were almost all there was. Mrs. Trent had sometimes caught in Nora's eyes the look of a scared little girl . . . a poor, sweet little thing she was in her heart, maybe. . . . But that was plain dreaming. The meanness part wasn't dreaming, but real, as real as the terrible thing she had to face now. She couldn't really get another job easy. She

was too old. And she hadn't hardly anything laid by . . .
no family to turn to. Mrs. Trent's hand relaxed its grip on
the doorknob, and as one yielding, unanchored to a strong
tide, moved to the tub. Nora stepped over the edge, holding to the old woman's hand with her wet one. Then she
stood erect and motionless in the middle of the floor.
Taking down the huge orchid-colored towel, Mrs. Trent
wrapped it around Nora's shoulders and body, began to
massage it, drying her. Lifting a corner she carefully
dried the face, neck and chin. Nora made no move except
to raise her arms to be dried underarm and along her
sides. She looked at Mrs. Trent long and steadily when
the job had been done to Nora's knees. Expressionless,
Mrs. Trent had gone about the job, moving in a slow
circle around the young woman. Now, neither spoke, and
Mrs. Trent stood holding the towel across her forearms.

"Those old knees too creaky to bend, Nanny?" Nora
stared at her, eyes raised slightly to impale the taller
woman's.

"I could get the stool and you could set your foot up
on—" Mrs. Trent said, her voice hoarse, barely aloud.
"That would be most simple."

"For *you*. Leave the stool where it is. And hurry."

Mrs. Trent let herself down slowly, remained
crouched, staring blindly at the deep pile rug, the
slender white feet, the gleam of deep red polish on the
long smoothly rounded toes. Then in a frenzy of speed
she scrubbed the legs dry from knees to heels, thinking.
"I'm scratching the skin, scratching it bleeding raw."

"That's the way, Nanny . . . put some heart in it. I like
to feel it . . . a good vigorous rub brings the skin glowing.
Thanks, dear . . . you're catching on so well."

Mrs. Trent looked up, trembling, her eyes swimming,
her face furious. Nora looked down at her, a set smile on
her lips. She touched the top of the woman's head. "Your
cap is all askew. You must try and be neat, dear. Be sure
and get between each toe. Nanny, you and I are going to
get along fine, aren't we?"

42

"Mmm."

"Aren't we? Look up and face me when you speak to me, dear."

"Yes." Mrs. Trent looked up again, then down quickly, mumbling, "If you'll raise this heel I'll be done."

"Yes? Did you say 'Yes'? Didn't you forget something?" Nora said, her voice little-girl sweet. "Look up at me, dear, and answer the way you should . . . we do want to understand each other, don't we, dear?"

"Yes, Ma'am."

"Yes ma'am we'll what?" Nora prompted. "Yes ma'am we'll understand each other?"

"Yes ma'am we'll understand each other."

"I know we will," Nora said coolly. "Now go back to bed, I want to be alone."

Alone in her bedroom, pulling off the bathing cap and letting the rich curly mass of reddish brown hair fall down around her slender white shoulders, Nora faced the long mirror. She cupped her small, firm breasts momentarily, then let her fingers trail sensually down her body, along the swelling contours of her hips, down her thighs, looking at the image of herself with dreamy eyes. She lowered the lids and let her mouth open slightly. She lifted her hands in front of her at chin level, palms toward her, the wrists bent back, the fingers semiflexed, extending petal-like, upward. Slowly, as one making an offering she extended her hands arms length toward the mirror. She bent her head to one shoulder, and then to the other, and watching herself avidly, began to sway gently from the hips from side to side, bringing her extended arms up and out overhead. She rose on the balls of her feet, her toes splaying, buried in the deep nap of the carpet. She stood motionless, body stretched upward, her breasts high. She tipped her head back, pointing her chin at an angle so that she could see the long tendon leading to the base of her throat stand out in a taut, delicate line.

She railed her fingers in the triangular hollow dipping

43

back of her clavicle from the base of her throat to the round of her shoulder. Pivoting, she posed in profile to the mirror, looking at herself over one shoulder. She stood flat on her heels, then rose on her toes, watching the subtle change in the line of her arched back curving in deeply at the waist, flaring out below, tapering in again to the straight clean line of thighs.

"How right he was," she thought, remembering the man at Freelands who had made a shrine. He had worshiped the image of her, and perhaps there had been something more profound in that than she knew. He hadn't needed greedy animal contact.

"Clean," she thought, "clean and pure and white."

She danced for herself, pirouetting, bending, swaying, silent and graceful. She whirled out across the room, running nimbly, making short leaps, turning, veering off along imaginary turning and twisting patterns. Yet there was restraint, almost a formality, and not for several minutes did the easy but controlled flow-line of her movements begin to break. Aware that she had begun to dance faster, she stopped before the mirror. Her breath was coming more quickly and the vigor of her movements had brought a glow to her eyes.

"A goddess," she whispered. "A goddess."

Her mind rebelled against the silence. She gave a short, exultant cry, ran to the wall switch and turned out the lights. From the partly opened bathroom door and the cross-slits of dim illumination through the venetian blinds a faint light reflected dimly in the mirrors, from the frosted and cut-glass dressing table bottles, from the heavy satin bedspread, from the leather and plastic chairs, from the flat orchid surfaces of the upper walls and ceilings. A breath of night air mingled with the heavy warmth of the room and a distant blur of traffic sound came in . . . the sound of the ocean . . . it began to drum against her mind, rising in volume, drumming hollowly, evenly, as waves broke; and she stood motionless, staring, breathing through her mouth. She stood

44

with her feet braced apart, listening as the beat rose. She held her hands curved clawlike and rigid in front of her. She thrust her hands wildly forward, her nails digging at the air, she ran forward.

The waves kept breaking in loud, driving thuds. Her motions became abrupt. Quick, violent thrusts of her arms, her legs. She stomped, she crouched. Her head drew back, shot out. In the dim, almost soundless room her breath came fast and loud in sharp inhales, gasping exhales. Then she began sloughing her palms against her flanks, striking in rhythmic, glancing blows, swinging her arms back and forth, brushing her hands against her legs in a gradually rising tempo, catching up to the beat of the breaking waves that continued to drum, drum, drum, swifter, racing ahead of her.

She stopped dancing and concentrated on trying to catch the racing, deep-hollow drumming of the waves with her hands . . . right, left, right, left, faster and faster, sloughing against her thighs, feeling the growing tingle in her flesh coming in waves one on the other, up and across and around her body more and more compellingly. She was not aware that her arms moved any longer, but the waves had silenced, the brush of her palms grew harder, their direction changed, the blows came no longer in side brushes; the feathery sluffs sharpened to slaps. The tingling in her flesh mounted like a slowly increasing current that at first seemed only like a delightful tickling over her skin, then increased, vibrating deeper and deeper into her flesh and through her body and limbs so delicately yet so persistently that it seemed to quiver in every fiber, and to sweep her irresistibly and completely into its grip. The situation became too wild; it was agony. She wanted to scream. She pitched face down onto the bed, her head toward the footboard. Reaching out she gripped the footboard in her clenching hands, legs outspread, her feet in the pillows. She lay rigid, holding on against the hot surging in her, fighting down the trembling tension of her body.

She remained for minutes without moving. When at last she rose, a little smile of triumph was on her face. She slipped into a nightgown and got under the covers. From the bed table drawer she took two sleeping tablets, swallowed them dry. She slept, the love ritual finished, the body set craving and not appeased. She was strong, she was pure. She woke at noon, sharply alert, angry. There had been a dream. It escaped her memory at once. She jabbed at the bell.

She looked silently at the old woman when she appeared, sat up, letting her feet over the side.

"I'm sorry for the way I've treated you, lately," Nora thought. "You have been humiliated enough."

And then The Gray Eyes were back again, watching her, and she said aloud:

"Hurry up and get my mules, do you think I'm going to step on this dirty carpet?"

She was glad The Gray Eyes were back. She could do as she pleased.

They were real, too. When they were in a body they belonged to Ed Harlon. After the fourth meeting with him at the park zoo, she had brought a private detective. She knew where he lived, where he worked. She went into the next room, sat at the little desk and wrote him a note while her bath was running.

CHAPTER V

"WELL, I AM GOING TOWARD MONEY," Ed thought as his scarred right palm started to itch maddeningly. Her note, a childish sprawl of spidery words on quiltlike lavender-tint vellum, was in his breast pocket. Nora Emlaine. "I don't like your name, either," he'd say. "That gives us something in common." That'd pull a laugh. He turned out of his street onto the avenue, heading for the subway. It was damp and chilly tonight, the sky hanging low and choked, its underside pink from the glow of midtown lights. "Ever notice the sky in this burg is pink—sometimes diluted orange," he'd toss off.

He veered out of the way of a girl moving on rapid high heels along the narrow outer strip of walk to avoid the open grill over the subway. A train growling deeply raced under him, thrusting gusts of stale hot air up into his face. He exhaled in an angry whoosh, feeling contaminated by the subway air, and ducked into a store for mints to freshen his mouth.

He stood crunching mints at the corner near the top of the subway steps, hands in his overcoat pockets, deciding whether to spend fifteen cents or a buck. He scanned with a disinterestedly superior eye the people who went into the subway. Did even one of them ever think of riding a cab? He shrugged them away. Little-thinkers, the lot of them.

He sauntered to the curb, turning his back on the subway. He lifted a finger at a cab. It sped on and he watched it disdainfully. Two more passed him, and then one pulled in. He entered, gave the address in a tone of boredom. "Think big, be big," he thought, riding uptown. He tipped the doorman who came out to the end of the marquee to open the cab door, letting the driver in on his familiar "How's everything tonight?" greeting.

From the moment the elevator doors purred shut at his back, the silence began to swallow him. He held his neck erect, his face matching the stiffness of the butler's man-of-distinction-ad face. The man didn't take his hat and coat or give any sign that Mr. Harlon was expected, only mumbled and vanished. He lighted a smoke, stuck the burnt match in his pocket. If she kicked him out, after a long think about him, and he had to go right back down, facing the elevator admiral and doorman, he'd have to get the guy to order him a cab. He wasn't going to walk away from there and give them any ideas about what kind of class he was.

47

He looked around with an air of casual proprietorship, watching the fanspread of an exhale as it dissolved in the queer misty light of the apartment. He sauntered to the threshold of the sunken living room. The entrance was spanned by a ten-foot arch. On either side were columns, like those in front of a bank, only painted gold. He touched one of the shafts thinking it was stone, but it was painted wood, hollow, he discovered, thumping. He nodded, thrusting out his underlip with an air of connoisseurship.

Two low, wide curving steps led down to the big room which looked like the lobby of a modernistic theater or museum. The carpet was supposed to be an ocean, with waves running across it in shades from pale to deep green. There were even jagged looking snaky strips of white along the crests. The ceiling had sunken oval panels with sloping sides of frosty blue glass over tube lights.

The far wall was an unbroken surface of pale yellow from ceiling to floor . . . drapes hanging motionless and heavy in a series of full even pleats, rolling in and out—but in the indirect light, no shadows filled the depressions. It gave a sort of deep look that was soft, but solid looking too. There'd be windows or French doors back of the drapes, he decided. The right wall was a checkerboard of alternating two-foot squares of glass brick and smoke-blue mirrors. In the middle of that wall was a plain white door with a standard glass knob . . . a real homey touch, he thought wryly. It was the left wall covered with a huge modernistic mural that out-weirded anything he ever saw. He looked and turned, looked and turned from it. Below the mural was a super-salon touch. A yellow leather seat ran its whole length, from the draped wall to this one. It was a fat affair too, the back rests bellying out and down, converging with the big bowing seat . . . maybe bed was the word.

Down in the angle formed by the draped wall and the glass-brick one was a truck-long grand piano painted

48

the same lemon color as the drapes. Mirror over the keyboard, he bet. Press a button, up pops Iturbi from the ocean carpet. Hell, Harlon went to the movies, kids, you couldn't fool Harlon. Across from the piano was a piddling little phonograph not worth a nickel over fifteen hundred dollars. Back of it, shelves built in the wall climbed back of glass doors with rows and rows of albums. Without binoculars he hadn't realized that the album section of the wall wasn't part of the mural. Around the phonograph were grouped sectional pieces of modern furniture, tables, ash stands, and chairs of glass, plastic, chrome, yellow leather, and carpet-matching ocean wave leather.

Nearer at hand, just a long spit out from the gold capped genuine imitation stone column on his left was another mood. Harem-ish. Low stools, ottomans, bushel-size squashy satin covered cushions in delicate bakery window pastels of pinks and lavenders and limes and peach. In the near corner, off the right column, was something else again. The boys' side. Really rugged and virile, that grouping. Four low, seriously squat, square, wide-armed leather chairs facing in from the points of a square. Clean boys, though—white leather. And, gracious, gracious, careless as boys will be: a two-inch scar where the leather had been ripped and sewed . . . and the complexion of another chair arm had suffered a burn —reminding him that his cigarette ember was getting too far toward his fingers. He went down the two steps to the amoeba shaped glass table within the four-chair square, mashed out his cigarette in a foot-long ash tray which was a replica of the gray, whale-bodied city garbage trucks.

Fascinated, he regarded the low table, a drunken affair that gave the illusion it was about to topple. It had only two legs, and he'd have sworn it was higher at the end supported by the thick, irregularly bulging transparent plastic leg which looked like a stocking full of potatoes. The near end was supported by a straw thin leg that looked like a case of compound fracture, shooting down to the base in an erratic zigzag line as though buckling under the weight. He pressed down experimentally on the glass top. Nohing tipped or broke. The garbage truck ash tray, box of cigarettes and lighter remained secure.

"Mrs. Emlaine will be with you presently," the butler said from the steps. Ed glanced at him, then back to the wall niche in the corner, seeing for the first time the work of art in the niche. It was an orange crate up-ended: a pair of holes bored through it—eyes; another hole—nose; a lipsticked mustache below that; below the outer corner of the mustache another hole—mouth. "A Square Fellow Talking out of the Side of His Mouth," was the title. He shrugged out of his coat, carried it and his hat to the butler, tipped a thumb toward the orange crate lop-faced figure in the niche.

"Who's the big talent back of that?"

"Mrs. Emlaine, sir."

Ed thumbed across his shoulder at the mural.

"Likewise, Mrs. Emlaine?"

"It's entitled The City," the butler said, nodding.

Ed nodded too, and bunching his brows thoughtfully, came to a decision. "Yes," he said. "The City." The butler was about to dismiss *him*. How the hell did you brush off a snooty bastard so he'd know who was brushing who? The guy was starting off down the short hall. Ed watched him go through a door, shut it silently.

He shrugged and went back down onto the oceanic carpet. He paced to the end of the room, touched the drapes, turned to the piano, resisted an impulse to plink one of the keys. No mirror over the keyboard . . . just a gag, he knew there wouldn't be. He went over, probed and found the center parting in the drapes, peered into the darkness through a section of glass French door, saw the dark mass of a near-by apartment top, looked down at the irregular pattern of lighted rectangles on its flanks, over it to the pink midtown sky, the familiar skyline, smeary and indistinct tonight—it was good to shut it out and breathe the rarefied air in here.

He went back and sat in one of the squat leather chairs, pulled out his pack, then changing his mind scooped a handful of cigarettes out of the box and put them in his breast pocket along with Nora Emlaine's note. The quiet hung over the place like something alive. Space and quiet. This is what the big shots bought. A big armor of insulated space. He looked overboard at the ocean floor . . . hell, they even fixed things so they could walk on water. Quiet and privacy all boxed up neat away from the masses, breathing their own air, nobody pushing or crowding them . . . no wonder they got to feeling like gods. Well, he could feel like that too if he had the equipment. Everything the city was this wasn't, he thought, looking at the big mural. The City! Where did she get the big impression? Maybe dipping one of those long legs down out of this stratosphere and wiggling a pink toe in the stream of life and feeling it tickle.

So what. He sat back and smoked and took his leisure like a squire. He wished Paul Chessly that ex-ham was getting a load of him. He felt expansive. He could even like Paul Chessly. Why not, in a layout like this? What's to bother anybody; what's to make anybody up in a roost like this mad at anything?

The queen was taking her time. He thought of her dressing somewhere back in the apartment, taking her own damn sweet time. She was screwy, the way she talked. But *how* she talked was what showed she was class. She never got her tonsils calloused learning to outshout the subway. A sweet lay with a swell layout, he thought, because that was the way he knew it was going to be. Hell, that was the way it had to be. She'd sent for him, hadn't she? Thought enough about him to find out how to reach him, even after that "I don't know you" act.

He got up and went over to the mural, eased his

weight down on one knee, listening to the polite exhalation of the upholstery, stood up. He paced before the painting, pursing his mouth, studying what he might say about it, figuring himself part of this new world that he would have to wise up in. He caught himself dealing himself in deeper than he had any right to, building a long run on what might only be a one-night stand. Still. . . . Resolutely he drew his thoughts back to the painting.

The 5-A Ad gang of fast-mouths would horselaugh his kind of painting. They'd never even begin to understand it. Or the average woman—take for example Edna—she wouldn't even know how to look at it, let alone paint it. He'd have to start studying up on art and getting around to museums and things. Tomorrow Paul Chessly'd give him the smirk and ask "How was it?" meaning just one thing, and pop off like he did when he saw the note and the address about how would it be to rub up to something made out of diamonds—pretty rough! The guy sure had moaned over those sour grapes. When he got set right he sure wanted to get Chessly up here and rub his nose in it.

The picture had a snarled and twisted feeling, that was it. Violent colors, jagged fierce twisted lines crossing and crisscrossing, and tongues of crested, spiny flame hurling down savagely into jumbles of fractured segments of circles, broken squares and triangles; wild dipping and looping lines streaking up and down, trailing off, twisting back; a scarlet streak through a barb-wire mass of electric blue rods; balls of flame splintering out in showers.

Lines thin as hair, broad and straight; lines bulging, lines swimming. Every color from blacks to whites, greens, purples, orange and pink; phosphorous streaks starting in arcs, then pitching down steeply; wheels, sprockets; one big pinwheel silver against a black field sending out foaming showers of small faces, hands, arms, torsos—some vivid flesh color, some gashed through with black or with blood. Buildings drawn with careful sharp lines with tiny straight windows giving out real looking yellowish light—but no building upright; some leaning, some upside down, some within wheels. Two—no, three —life-size faces of beautiful women, clear and real as regular portraits. Busses, trains, distorted and abstract, swollen then thin, their outlines blurred, and made up of as many as ten separate colors, each running a little way, then chopping off to an opposite color. A white cigar with ember submerged in an upside-down stein of beer with purple smoke rising through the glass bottom, then cascading in a blue stream down a flight of steps. Whew! He peered closer, and then saw something for the first time!

The whole surface of the mural was overlaid very faintly with wave-lines, like the carpet, but very pale green. But the waves were from top to bottom, like an ocean on its side. The waves weren't distorted the way everything else was. They ran evenly from the edge of the glassed in album shelves clear to the front wall. Maybe he was getting something from it, at that, he thought, scratching his scarred palm. The even smoothness of those waves in contrast with the senseless jumble of the city . . . like the city was under the waves without even rippling their surface—like the whole works was drowned, dead and gone down under the water. He scratched his jaw. He shrugged, puzzled about the whole works. Take the average guy, he thought, and he'd get no meaning out of art like this. Me, he thought, I really am getting a big feeling. It communicates to me, he thought, and stood self-consciously and blankly contemplating the mural and seeing himself as artistic, just a touch suave, a little contemptuous of the Paul Chesslys, the phony posers like that.

He turned. She was standing across the room by the white door, a hand resting lightly on the glass knob.

"Good evening," he said. "I was just admiring your pictures, Mrs. Emlaine." .

She came across the room, smiling, wordless, waiting

53

for him to finish and he knew he'd get his tongue in a trap if he wasn't careful. "It hits you," he said lamely. "Real feeling. It's the kinda thing you have to take slow." A magic word picked up somewhere, sometime, came to his lips. "Vibrations. Such tremendous vibrations."

"You should like it. It's you. Isn't it?"

"I guess you'd say that . . . a feeling of vibrations there between us . . . like it speaks out to me. . . ." Jeez, he was spieling as good as if there was a phone up to his kisser or else a few double shots in his belly. "It gripped me from the minute I stepped in . . . seemed to reach out and pull me."

The words were gushing in him . . . dynamic, vivid, impact, tonality, composition . . . he could've spieled them as if he were talking to a guy who had just asked for the page rate instead of inch rate, but it hit him that she was wise to him and pulling his leg half out of the socket.

". . . I don't know how many people have known how that picture spoke to them, and, God, it had said everything to them from Modern Love, Modern Housing and Social Protest to The Indecipherable Omnipresent Futility of Life. But you do know it, it's you, and later sometime you can explain it to me."

He laughed loudly. "You're sharp," he said. Sharp was a specialized 5-A word meaning everything from beautiful and brilliant to so-so or lousy. Sometimes, as now, it meant simply: "You know I wouldn't kid you, you know what I really meant."

"Can't let you in on any secrets, can I?" he continued. It was more 5-A jargon. It gave him a certain sense of comfort and security to talk the foreign language to her while she was figuring him for a dope, an outsider that she was amusing herself with. It passed her. She said:

"We'll sit down. I'll do the talking. There's so much I've got to say. Then we'll go into you, about that name— and that body—I've been wondering about it."

"That," he thought, "goes double." She looked him up and down in a detached way that was neither approving nor critical. It was—well, as she said, wondering. He felt a little uncomfortable.

He returned her scrutiny, but without the same detachment. She wore wide-bottomed black lounging pajamas. The blouse was loose, high and closed at the throat, long sleeved. Her feet were enclosed in deep, flat heeled slippers of foamy black alpaca. The pajamas were heavy velvet, and though fitted trimly with a wide band at the waist and flowing in a long, sinuous line, they certainly weren't enticing. Maybe they were, he supposed, or they would be if she was made up right. But she wore no rouge or lipstick, and her hair fell down along her cheeks casually, and a little untidily. Of course she was pretty, but without color her lips didn't look good, especially in this light. She hadn't taken any pains about his coming, that was certain, although he'd been a little slow catching on.

There was a subtle challenge about her refusing to glitter herself. Sort of an arrogance about it that excited him. As if she knew she was so desirable that he or any man would have to take her on her own terms. As if she had deliberately made herself worse, knowing a guy would yield no matter how she was. He could barely keep his hands off her. But she was setting the pace. She wanted to talk, so she'd talk. He'd wait.

And yet there was something directly opposite about her. A submissive look, a way of hesitating and looking at him . . . as if . . . as if she were waiting for him to tell her what to do next, as if he had a secret password or a cue she had to have. He waited for her to do the talking she said she would do. But she went over to the piano and stood there and looked down at the keyboard and looked over at him. He walked over, and the way she watched him gave him the willies. He got the notion that she was trying to figure out who he was, and then when he was closer and she kept looking, he saw she

55

knew him all right and expected him to speak or make a move that they both knew . . . something . . . something . . . as if she were not only very much at home and at ease and familiar witth him but that he was the leader in some private game, and she couldn't move till he did.

He stepped close to her, looked down in her face. He knew the move all right. His hand slid quickly about her back. He pulled her tight against him and bent, kissing her mouth. He felt her back tauten, the firm bands of muscles flanking her spine quickening to life under his palm. He pressed harder, and she writhed against him. She turned her face and bent back. He ran his other hand up through her hair and cupped the back of her skull firmly and turned her face and kissed her mouth again, and she twisted her head in the other direction, and a gasp escaped her lips. He kissed her again, but his mouth touched her cheek instead of her lips. She had her hands up, her fists clenched to his lapels, and she was pushing with all the strength of her arms. He held his arm and hand locked around her back, the other holding her head. She was arched back, her chin straight up, her neck muscles pushing back against his grip; her fist thrusts pushing steadily out against his chest. Her hips turned from side to side, wildly, all of her fighting him. He couldn't pull her face back. She had her lips flattened to her gums and her teeth clenched and he let her go, and stood breathing hard, looking at her savagely. She stared, her lids close together, her lips mashed whitely together, breathing swiftly, the sides of her nose compressing slightly and relaxing out. A faint sheen of sweat had come over her face, her breasts rose high and fell, but she stood with her arms hanging limply, and her body began to relax, and he saw the pink tip of her tongue moistening her lips and her eyes blinked a few times and returned to normal. She clenched her fist and struck the keys of the piano, looking down at them, then back at him. He

56

frowned as he realized no sound had come from the struck keys.

"I'll go," he said stiffly.

She lifted her hand, waved it casually sidewise. "Have a drink. I'll send for ice."

The lid of the piano had come up. The inside was a bar.

"I'll be damned," he said. "I thought it was a real piano."

"It was," she said. "I cut the strings."

"You mean on purpose?"

"I pounded them with an ash tray and the legs of a chair; I tried nail scissors, a butcher knife and big scissors and nothing worked and I tore my nails and fingers damned near to pieces and I was going around sobbing I was so furious, but I took a few drinks and thought about it and sent out for wire clippers from a hardware store and then I had an afternoon of it. One string at a time. I'd take a sip out of a drink and say here's to you, Johann Sebastian—then WHING . . . the damn thing would leap up like an eel in an electric socket, scratching and clawing the lid till it had to be refinished. Then a sip and here's to YOU, Wolfgang Amadeus—WHING . . . and to hell with *you*, Chopin . . ." She broke off, giggling.

"Well," Ed said, looking at the display of liquors, "you really turned the piano into an instrument I can go for."

"I did, eh?" she said, coldly. "I did? You think I did, eh?"

CHAPTER VI

As she talked and watched him she arrayed herself for him. She felt a little troubled and uncertain but she did not let him see it. She sat cross-legged, holding her ankles in her fingers under her knees, upper body erect, facing him. Sometimes she turned sidewise, half-lying on hip and thigh, half-sitting, her body leaned, supported by her arm on the low back of the curved sectional piece. Or she would tuck her legs under, sitting primly tall on her heels, her hands clasped on her lap. Once when his eyes had disconcertingly climbed past her up the album shelves at her back, she had lain on her back, her head down over the end of the seat, letting her hair fall away from her face to the carpet so that he could see the delicacy of her ears, and the loveliness of her throat line in that position. He saw her naked and beautiful, always, and always he had to feast on the variations of her position, relishing each new shifting of balance, every play of muscle.

He had asked, pretending not to understand that she had created him, and she was explaining their relationship. He had said he was not sure that *she* knew, and so she must talk and prove to him that she did.

". . . you watch, and you know, and you listen as I tell you . . ." she said, "and when I have done a wrong, you scold . . ." She paused as he leaned out to take a cube of ice from the bowl on the table, lift it with the tongs into his glass. She set her feet on the floor while he unstoppered the cut-glass decanter, poured whisky on the ice. She pressed her knees together, her legs and feet neatly together, pressed close so that she could feel the anklebones touching through her pajamas. She leaned forward resting her arms on her legs, looked down at her hands cupped on her knees. As she heard him settle back in the triangular sectional seat and knew his eyes were again on her, she looked up at him under her lids and resumed talking. "And you forgive the wrongs I do. You see that I do not tire from carrying them, because I must be free and happy and never tired from carrying them . . ."

He lifted his glass and shifted his eyes down away from hers, so she stopped talking. She extended her left

58

foot, and bent it down from the ankle until a slit of white skin appeared between pajama leg and the black alpaca slipper. She heard the ice clunk dully against the thick glass as he lowered it, and she looked to see his eyes watching, unblinking gray watching, and talked. ". . . so that there will be no heaviness in me, no tears . . . so that you will carry them for me . . . when I have done a wrong it will be yours. I will talk it to you and you will scold and forgive and carry it with you because you are so strong . . ."

A sting of excitement was in her. She rolled her shoulders, leaned back and began to raise and lower her legs from the knees, touching the carpet with her slippers, straightening each leg as though they were shears. She laced her fingers back of her head, looking obliquely up at the ceiling, squinting her eyes, then opening them wide to make the frosty sifts of light through the ovals of glass blur moistly and then come sharp-edged clear again. There was an exultant note of laughter, of buoyancy in her voice as she talked.

Then suddenly it all went flat.

Words, words, words. Such were words, she thought. Such they were, the masks, the lies, the disguises. The more Nora talked of their relationship, the less she could believe in it. It was such that it was understood wordlessly, or it was not so. And she knew it was not so. But back in her mind, way, way back, she had a desperate longing to make it so. It even crossed her mind—though she repudiated the thought immediately—that maybe if she just held him, as she knew she could, by his interest in her body, she could make him be what he should be. Her eyes sought his gray ones and were disappointed to find not the calm that should have been there, but a craftiness and a heated desire. With her disappointment was a feeling of excitement that she fought down. When he had come, when she had again seen him she had known that this creation was not a fact. It did not survive contact. There had been other creations—in music

59

and painting, in dancing, in friendships—in love, even—as with the others, this one did not hold together when it became real. Her world had nothing in common with the flesh. Hers was another world. This one was a horrid farce, she knew. Even before he had put his hands and his mouth on her she had known.

She talked on, making the game for him to play, putting it in world-words, knowing that he was a nobody, a not even bright sort of commonplace person who wanted to go to bed with her, who was pretending to humor her, who was scornful of her talk . . . scornful and a little disturbed, maybe even horrified of her. And he was moving along according to her lead, like some flaccid hulk, afraid to laugh aloud, afraid to express his real contempt, his real opinion. He thought he was humoring her, that he would get something out of it.

And yet, despite a sense of excitement, a sense of control, a sense of triumph at winning a sort of contest, there was an uneasiness, a sort of aching undercurrent. Because to know he was just Ed Harlon, a commonplace on-the-make male, was to admit her own flaw. She hadn't the imagination, hadn't the strength of intellect and will to create a world that would defy the contemptible, stupid, ugly and cruel one accepted by the mass. She lacked the power to slam a door on it.

"I think," Nora said, "I understand the reason for your body, now. I think you are even more than my creation. Because I was never able to make you materialize of my own will, was I? Perhaps you *couldn't* materialize while Mr. Emlaine was alive . . . or you wouldn't, maybe that's it. You wouldn't because when you did materialize you would want me all to yourself."

She stopped and smiled at him. "Is that so, Ed?"

She sighed as he nodded, his face a blank. She watched him lean out again for more whisky. "There was some will or force that you alone had, Ed. Only with your consent would you have materialized. A mating of our wills, wouldn't you say. Your contribution was the flesh,

60

the body—of course, as a man that would be your contribution—the body. To love and worship me and serve me . . ."

"Love 'n worship 'n serve, huh?" he said. "What're you sitting there for? Come on my lap . . ."

"But I haven't finished. You may think I don't really know what our relationship is."

"Sure, you know. I give you A plus. . . . C'mere, darling. Didn' you say you obey me?"

"Yes, of course, when your eyes are talking . . . that part I obey, when I've done a wrong and you scold; but the body can't interfere, of course."

"You just obey your part of me, what you want to, huh?"

She smiled, nodded brightly. "So there will be no heaviness and tears for me to carry. You will carry them. When I've done a wrong it will be yours. You will scold and forgive and we will be happier than ever because you are flesh and I'll be able to see you carry the weight. It is better than when you didn't have a body. Now, when I give you the weight to carry it won't fall where it can't be seen in the air. To see you flinch and bend under the weight will make it clear to me how free and strong I am. Nobody else is free, nobody else will know how fine it is to watch their burdens carried. It won't be abstract any more. It will be fun to hurt."

"You'll like doing the wrong things, then, huh?"

"Of course. It's fun to hurt people and then it isn't, because it becomes a feeling that is heavy, or sometimes it is sharp and pointed; and then it can hurt me. And so . . . so . . . I make words out of the feelings and you listen to them. You used to listen to them with your eyes when you hadn't a body . . . you listen to them. It will be different now, the words. When I made feelings into words and whispered them the eyes saw them, but now they're not just vapor coming out that you can see . . . you can hear too. And your flesh can feel them. . . ."

"You'll always be free then to do any damned thing

61

you please," Ed said, and he wasn't really drunk, he felt. Not really drunk at all.

"That way . . ." she began. She felt confused. She wanted to say, "That way, I am always clean and pure and beautiful, because there isn't any badness in me, the badness is yours, I give it to you and I stay happy because happiness is beauty, beauty is happiness, is good, is beauty, is happiness . . . never worry, never tears, never regrets . . . that is what you are . . . that that . . ." But the things that were so did not need words between them. The Gray Eyes understood, The Gray Eyes, seeing her always naked and beautiful and pure. They had a body now.

"I suppose," she said, "you think my talk is stupid. You must be hungry . . ."

"I must be," he said. "I get that way looking at you . . . well, you're not going to push me off when I kiss you now, are you?" He got to his feet.

She didn't answer. He sat beside her. When his hand touched her she sprang to her feet. She turned and looked down at him. She pressed her palms tightly against her flanks. He reached for her and she stepped back, waited, watching him get up. She stood, holding her hands hard against her legs. A slow tickling, like small feathers, had begun to brush her skin. There was a set, humorless grin on his face, and his eyes watched intently as he came to her. His fingers touched the loose sleeve of her blouse and she darted sideways. She went to the piano-bar and pressed one of the bell-buttons affixed to it.

Nora saw him frown and pause as she rang for the butler, but he came to her again. The tickling shivered up and down her body. It gave her a feeling of terror, and she knew she must not be touched. He must not touch her. He must not be told. He could not be told. He must know without words that something horrible, something vague and hidden but horrible would happen if he touched her. She pressed her hands harder against her legs, standing transfixed, communicating it to him with her eyes.

He was very near, and nothing about his gray eyes yielded to what she was communicating. They stared through and into the back of her mind and read something. They did not listen to the silent words she was saying, but ignored them. His hands lifted and pressed her cheeks and hair, holding her head, drawing her face forward. She smelled the fumes of whisky on his breath, and worked her tongue and cheeks trying to gather saliva. She must spit in his face. But his mouth mashed against hers, covering her lips, holding fast against them. His hands pressed tighter, locking her head, pressing her hair in a hard mass that hurt her ears and muffled outer sound so that she could hear the blood like some terrible, distant humming.

He was hurting her head and her lips and she was strangling for breath. Her fingers curved, held like rigid claws beside her. Her hands edged forward, and she thought she must maim him; that she must fasten her claws in him and hold while he cried out in agony and beat her off. She would hold relentlessly while his fists beat her face, and breasts. She would withstand the bruising, the pain, while his bony knuckles smashed into her. She would laugh and take all the punishment he could give, and she would not yield, not until she was knocked unconscious.

But her hands remained clawed, motionless. She remained otherwise passive. His tongue probed into her mouth in a French kiss and her teeth poised, ready to clamp and hold, locked mercilessly. He would gasp with the pain, but he would be helpless, and in a fury would strike her in the stomach and the ribs. He would bludgeon her head, and try to wrench free, but she would hold her jaws locked, and sink her teeth through the flesh until they met. He would flounder and throw the pair of them crashing to the floor, trying to pull away from her, but he would be fastened, unable to free himself. He would pull her hair, but it would be he who screamed in agony as his pinioned tongue was jerked. He would fasten his arms around her and press with all his strength, cracking her ribs, trying to mash the air and the life out of her, and she would not release him. He would clamp her throat in his fingers and strangle her until a veil of red came across her eyes, and he would press his thumbs deeper into her windpipe until the redness dimmed and blackened away into unconsciousness. She stood passively receiving his kiss, and after an eternity she saw his face detached from her, and she rubbed her tingling lips with the palm of her hand and stared into the intensity of his gray eyes and said nothing. The butler announced himself quietly, and she said:

"We'll want a little lunch. Mrs. Trent may serve it."

She wanted Nanny. She had to have her here. "My foot-servant!" she thought. Now, more intensely than she could remember, she wanted the old woman there, wanted her serving, taking orders, accepting with cowed docility her role. Now, The Gray Eyes could watch, could listen to her tone of voice in speaking to the gray-haired old creature.

Nora excused herself and went into her bedroom, then into her bathroom. She looked at the tub, "No, not time," she said aloud. "I will wash my hands and face." She filled the basin, turning on both jets, leaning braced on her hands, looking down at them under the roily water, listening to the deepening thrum of the water as the swift streams buried deeper and deeper into the rising water. She let the jets continue full force when the bowl was overflowing, and stood, looking down, watching the overflow spilling into the open grating of the drain. Then she stood straight, swept her hair back with both hands. She secured it with one hand at the nape of her neck and bent her face down to the swirling surface of the water, and slowly immersed. She pushed her face into the water, eyes open, and held it there till the pressure of her held breath began to burn in her chest. She exhaled explosively under the water, then stood straight and looked at her wet, dripping face in the mirror, feeling faint and dizzy. She stood regaining the evenness of her breathing and then dried her face.

She went back to the door between her bedroom and the front room, and pressing her ear listened. She waited until she knew Nanny had come. Standing there alone in the silent dark bedroom The Gray Eyes were very real. For awhile, in Ed Harlon's presence, she had doubted herself. There had been an instant of clarity when he had begun to kiss her. A raw clarity that flashed sharply and vanished. She had seen him detached from The Gray Eyes. She had seen him as a male who had excited her, whom she had deliberately picked up, who had nothing really to do with The Gray Eyes. She had wanted him simply because she had wanted him as a male . . . because he had been with another woman . . . because she wanted to love him . . . because . . . But the sharp instant of clarity had vanished.

She opened the door. Nanny was setting a large tray on a table. Nora moved toward her. She paused, stepped out of one slipper. She kicked the slipper away from her and said:

"Nanny!"

She saw Ed Harlon stare at her curiously, then at the slipper, then at her bare foot. Mrs. Trent looked at Ed.

"I spoke to you, Nanny. Look this way."

Mrs. Trent turned her head.

"Do I have to tell you to get my slipper and put it on?"

Ed walked over, picked up the slipper. He handed it to her, staring. Nora looked past him, dangling the slipper on her fingers.

"Don't think you're going to slink away, Nanny."

"My name's not Nanny, Mrs. Emlaine."

"What's that? I say your name is Nanny," Nora said. "And I am waiting."

65

"You expect her to put your shoe on for you?" Ed said.

"I expect obedience. Instant obedience," Nora said. She tossed the slipper contemptuously onto the floor. She snapped her fingers.

Mrs. Trent stared hostilely at her without moving. "What are you snapping at?"

"Stop showing off for Mr. Harlon. You know what I mean when I snap. And you know what you do about it."

Ed watched the color flush into the old woman's face. He bent and picked up the slipper again. "Can't you put on your own shoe . . . hell, I'll do it for you. Here, stick your leg out."

"This is a matter of principle," Nora said. "This old woman is my servant and she'll do as I say."

Ed turned to Mrs. Trent.

"All right," Nora cried. "Turn to her! Now, old lady, you're fired. Do you hear? You're fired, and that's that. You'll crawl to get back. You'll crawl right now . . . you HEAR. . . ."

"I been waiting to hear you fire me!" Mrs. Trent said. "That's what I been waiting to hear. I just wanted you to say it. I just wanted you to show yourself off, young Missy. Now, you showed yourself plain as can be. I sure am glad somebody got to see it." She turned to Ed. "You maybe didn't know she was in an insane asylum. No, she never told that, I bet you. You're new, and she would keep it from you. The people that used to come here all knew it. Only nobody comes now that the Mr. is dead. Nobody comes any place near her."

"It's your last chance. I said *Crawl* . . . and beg, you hear, old woman, you HEAR? Come crawling and begging . . . I mean literally, old woman, down on your knees. I'll count ten. One . . . two . . . and when you get here begging you'll kiss my feet . . . three . . . four . . . do you HEAR? . . . five . . . six . . . and THEN I'll turn you over my knees and spank you, do you understand it? Yes, I'll tan you, and right in front of company too, and send you crying off to bed with a lesson you'll not forget . . . seven . . . eight, you'll have to lick my hands like a dog . . . lick my FEET . . . do you HEAR? Come. Come crawling and take your medicine. You have been impudent and I don't allow that. Come. CRAWL . . ."

"It's worse than I ever heard," Mrs. Trent said. She shook her head. "I got another job, Mrs. Emlaine. Even if I never had one I'd not stay around you a minute more."

Nora's mouth fell open. She stared. She started toward Mrs. Trent. She had a look on her face that made the old woman back off a step, involuntarily, and look in stunned horror at her. Nora felt Ed's hand fasten around her arm. She yanked loose. She moved another step toward Mrs. Trent, ducking her head slightly. The woman stepped quickly to the side, around the table and over toward the wall seat. She started to hurry along it toward the end of the room. Nora was two yards from the bench, but between Mrs. Trent and the exit. "You're not going to get away, Nanny," Nora said softly. She felt the harsh grip of Ed Harlon's fingers on her shoulders. She lunged, but his hands held her and Mrs. Trent went swiftly past, out of reach.

Nora shrugged.

When she turned around to Ed he let his breath come out in a long, slow whistle. She had a look on her face that somehow gave him a mule kick in the gut. It was soft and gentle . . . like . . . his mind fumbled for a comparison. Star-eyed. A little girl. Yes. That was it. Like a scrub-faced, Sunday-good-behavior girl who has maybe just finished singing a pretty little song and is waiting to be praised and petted by the grown-ups.

He looked, incredulous, at her face. The things she had said, done; the fury, the cruelty . . . the . . . He looked past her head to her mural, then back at her.

"You were in an asylum?"

"Sanitarium. A lovely rest. So nice there, and I was

67

away from this . . . all of this . . . away from the late Mr. Emlaine . . . away from all of them . . ."

"When did they . . ." It was on his tongue to say: "When did they let you out?" but it had a sort of bluntness to it that he couldn't use. "When did you leave the rest place?"

"Last September," she said.

He nodded, opened his mouth, closed it.

"Yes," she said, answering his unspoken question. "My husband was alive then."

"Then—then you're just recently a widow?"

"Christmas morning . . . about 3 A.M."

"Oh . . . well . . ."

"If you want to see, I'll show you where he was hanging in the bathroom."

Suicide! He stared at her. "No," he said hoarsely. "I don't want—" He broke off, finished the sentence with slow shakes of his head. He looked again at the mural. How long ago was it he'd been thinking there was no conflict in this layout . . . no conflict . . . She was staring up at him, and he felt his palm begin to itch. There was an awful feeling in his chest, an aching, a sharp, hot aching. Just conflict enough to make a guy kill himself.

"You know," she said, moving casually over and taking a cube of cheese on a toothpick. "I am not insane. I haven't ever been declared insane. I wouldn't have minded it. Not really, except for being locked up for good. I've thought about having myself declared insane." She put the cheese in her mouth, remembering for a moment why she'd thought about having herself officially committed. It had seemed a fair way of locking up Mr. Emlaine; he couldn't have got a divorce as long as she lived . . . but she had abandoned that foolish notion. To be free and happy didn't go with official imprisonment. There had even been a time when Nora had seriously wanted psychiatric help, had wanted to be normal. She smiled bitterly at the word. Normal! She watched Ed Harlon take a sandwich, pour a stiff drink.

He barely tasted the sandwich. He was watching her, thinking. Wondering. Wondering. She was rich.

He finished the big drink in a single draught. He poured more. She sat cross-legged, eating, her attention absorbed by the trayful of food. He sipped at the drink, took one of the cigarettes he'd got from the box, lighted it. He drank his glass empty, poured again. He studied his scarred hand. He had a feeling he would like to tell her about himself, his own life. He had a feeling that there was something fine about her, something warm and gentle, something in need of protection. He wondered how rich she really was. Hell, if she liked to play The Gray Eyes game, he would go along. He'd listen and he'd scold and see her naked and beautiful and pure, always—wow!

"I wonder if she's packing?" Nora said.

"Who's that, darling?" he asked, abstractedly.

"Nanny," she said. "She thinks she's going to leave here."

"Well . . ." He didn't know what to think, but suddenly his mind was made up. "Let her go," he said. "What've you got me for, to love and worship and serve that beautiful white, naked, pure body for? You don't need anybody around but me. When are we going to be alone, baby?"

"She's got another think coming to her," Nora said.

Her little girl's face was twisted with spite. He stopped, changed pace, but he didn't take another drink.

"Sure," he said. "Sure."

He thought of the scummy jobs he'd had. He looked around the room and he looked at her. What if she had been sick? She was all right now. Hell, she was more than all right. What was more, she needed him. He looked at her again and this time found her eyes. They were those of a little girl, violet and soft and touchingly innocent. He let his own gray eyes probe into hers understandingly.

He didn't make the mistake this time of moving to-

69

ward her or touching her, and when she said, "You'd better go now," he said, "Sure."

He wasn't certain he'd be back. Only he was. Things were working out right. Things were clicking along in the groove. He felt like Paul Chessly. Better. Like an ex-Paul Chessly. Moving on and up.

CHAPTER VII

AFTER ED HARLON HAD LEFT, NORA paced quietly for more than an hour. She paused occasionally—once to close the piano-bar. Another time she carried over the garbage-truck ash tray with its ashes and mashed out cigarettes and set it on the step beside the column at the entrance. She brought the other trays from the far end of the room, put them alongside the big one. She found a burnt match, some cracker crumbs beside the chair he'd used most of the evening, carried them to the ash trays. Glasses, ice bowl half full of water in which ashes floated, the food remnants and plates on the tray were all removed to the step. She didn't set out to tidy the room. But little by little the evidences of his visit were obliterated. Sometimes she brushed at the blouse or pants of her pajamas. Sometimes she scrubbed her lips with the back of her hand.

She got a cigarette and went over to sit smoking it on the step beside the dirty ash trays. She smoked it through, staring vacantly at the surface of the carpet. Then she rose again and paced. Now and then a little frown would cross her face and she would stand still, looking down at the carpet, and try to think what it was she had been thinking about the moment before.

The thoughts came in short broken chains. They seemed to concern nothing in particular. She would be thinking about an apple tree and what month the blossoms came and then a sailor once on her father's boat telling what the hawse line and hawse hole was and the sailor's name had been Adam and Eve . . . just Adam, his name was . . . on that cruise to Cuba when the woman with her father had said: "On the island, girls of twelve . . ." Her father, red in the face, hearing and saying: "I forbid that kind of talk to her . . ." "Oh, you do? Well, it's true, girls her age . . ." "I am warning you . . . Nora, run along to your cabin."

No particular thoughts. None of them hanging together. A son is first and always a son . . . that was the best . . . before he is a father he is a son. Not mother knows best; grandmother is boss. . . . Some day Grandma will die and he will not be the son, just the father. . . . Then when we cruise we won't come back . . . we won't ever see her again or if Adam is fired. . . .

Ralph Emlaine will make a fine husband, Gran says, Gran knows. . . . Do you love me yes I do always a queer child a little unsettled . . . all dead now . . . Gran and father and Mr. Emlaine and Gran and father and Mr. Emlaine and once upon a time there was a great monster with the body of a fish and the wings of a bird and the head of a lion which came into the village and with a sweep of its tail made the house fall down and all of the children and the poor old grandmother were eaten alive and the great monster flew into the air and dove into the sea and for twelve years the great monster swam and then the great captain overtook the great monster and sent a harpoon in its head and out came the children and the grandmother going along the rope from the harpoon to the ship hand over hand and there was a great feast and the house in the village was rebuilt again and there was great rejoicing as the wedding was made between the captain and the fairest of the girl children, now grown to womanhood. . . .

She is quite a clumsy child and unmannerly and disobedient and she is not clean, nor will she sit still and she learned swear words and will spit and hiss when she is washed and I think I will have to send her away because she is vicious. . . . The dog whimpers and begs grandma for food and grandma does not know why . . . and one day she does know why . . . coming in as Nora scoops the meal out of the dog's pan and washes it away down the sink and then. . . .

Nora massaged her scalp, standing frowning down at the floor.

My little adorable girl wife; nothing will ever make you unhappy. I will be your daddy and your husband no matter if. . . .

Just as tall as the edge of the sink, the water running, washing the gooey mass of the dog's dinner down the drain; the dog on his hindfeet beside her pawing at her ribs, and then a scream and black and red lights in front of her eyes and her hair coming out of her head almost as she was caught by it and jerked backward and falling on the floor and then on her hands and knees, squeezed between Gran's legs, her bottom to the front. The dog standing looking at her from back of Grandma while she was getting her spanking, listening to the yelling and screaming. Another time caught, later, standing in the pan of dog food watching Gran's dog eat his dinner licking it off her feet and getting picked up by the hair and pulled off her feet and picked up and set down and picked up again by the hair.

Visits from her father when she would climb on his lap and be read to and told how pretty and sweet and wonderful and smart a little girl she was and Gran walking around the other side of the room and not leaving and always watching and always telling something: ". . . she pee-ed in my dog's water," ". . . she stole from the Sunday School collection." "Did you do those things, baby?" "Yes, I'm bad, take me away." "Yes, take her away." "Take me with you." "No, she'll stay here . . . I'll make her into something . . ." "Why are you naughty with Gran, baby?" "I like to be." "But not any more—

72

promise?" "I promise." "She'll think of something worse."
"Yes, I guess I will." "Promise you won't do such things
and I'll bring you something nice." "I promise. But she'll
take it away from me." "You mustn't say that."

Nora crossed the room and lay flat on her back on the
wall seat. She lay frowning, trying to remember what
she'd been thinking about.

Four years ago Stella Masters had come here blam-
ing her because Karl was in love with her. "My best
friend . . ." Nora smiled. Who but Stella would want
Karl. "Deliberately you did it, deliberately, you knew
what you were doing . . . now I want to know just how
far it's gone . . ." "All the details?" "You know what I
mean." "Well, it didn't go that far." "You're lying, Nora
Emlaine. God damn you, I'll claw that smug face of
yours to ribbons . . ." "I wouldn't lie to you, Stell." "Are
you sitting there telling me you didn't deliberately . . ."
"No." "You admit you made him fall in love with you?"
"Yes." "God damn you! . . . all right, I want to know the
WHOLE truth." "It didn't go the limit. He pawed me,
and he got down on his knees in front of the chair you're
in, and he kissed my palms and looked at me like a sick
dog and whined and begged and said he couldn't live
without me and then he kissed my palms again and began to say I was the only thing in the world, that he
worshiped and adored and loved and dreamed and
agonized and exalted and prayed and please, please,
please beautiful Nora, please make me happy, please
don't torture me any longer. Do you want to hear any
more, Stella?" "No . . . you dirty little . . ." "I said:
'Karl, I don't know what you're thinking about. I'm
married and you're married and Stella is my best friend
and of course I wouldn't betray her.' He said I had led
him on, and he became very angry and he prowled
back and forth over the room, and I waited for him to
calm down and he did, and came and began to whine
some more. I had to laugh, finally. He's all yours,
darling. But maybe you'd better keep him away from

me. Get him off some place alone, darling, where you won't have to compete . . . and good-by, darling . . . good- . . ."

She had said good-by to several friends that way. It was simple. The men couldn't resist the promise of something free. All mush, all ready to betray after a few lingering looks, after a well-timed secret hand squeeze or so, after a little display of interest, a few invitations with her body during a dance.

She sat up abruptly on the wall seat, lay back against the upright, hands folded across the top of her head. She hadn't any desire to sleep; no desire to do anything. She couldn't sit still. She went to the phonograph, lifted the door of an album shelf. Without even looking she got out one of the albums, set the records on the record changer, started the music.

She heard the opening measures and recognized them as a Stravinsky Suite, and then didn't listen any more. She thought of Nanny. She got another cigarette and sat on the steps, smoking by the ash trays. She held out her hand, seeing if it was steady. It trembled. She stood up and stretched her arm, hand reaching straight out, palm down, tried to hold it motionless. It wavered. She drew a long breath and paced a few steps out into the room, drawing on her cigarette, frowning.

She thought nothing at all. She was blank. She could hear the music dimly at the far end of the room and she walked to it, and turned up the volume. The discords crashed out at her, and she stood looking down at the spinning turntable, her mouth pulled back, lips hard against her teeth. She tensed and relaxed her shoulders and shivered. She snapped off the music, then spun around and stood, teetering, her eyes glazed, looking starkly across the space without seeing anything. Something crowded inside of her, something goading, aggravating, something stirring and pushing, something—just a feeling. She wiped her hand hard across her mouth and went toward the ash trays and tray of dishes, thinking she'd remove them. Then she looked down at them blankly when she was at the steps, and frowned, not remembering what she had wanted to do with them.

Something very funny about them. So untidy. She had started to clean up, and how careless, she scratched at a sudden itching on her cheek and then grinned, because her finger was wet . . . tears falling . . . she laughed aloud. She walked to the amoeba-shaped table, got out another cigarette, chain lighted it, spilling ashes. Then she hurried into her bedroom, got a cleansing tissue, came back and dusted the ashes from the table, crumpled and dropped the tissue to the carpet.

Drunk, he had got drunk. He had got thick-tongued, stupid drunk. He was gone, he had been just a man, just a commonplace pickup, and there were no gray eyes. There was nothing, anywhere, to be trusted.

She ran suddenly again into her bedroom, opened the bed table drawer, took out the sleeping pills. She took one. Then on an impulse, another. She slid out of her pajamas, got under the sheet. She lay waiting for sleep. She looked at the small clock. Two-twenty. Sleep didn't come. Two-thirty. She lay holding her eyes shut, body motionless. Her eyes jumped open. Two-forty. She closed her eyes. The minutes ticked past. She stayed motionless but alert, more and more alert. She looked at the clock. Two fifty. At 3 A.M. she had murdered him. She had killed. She had prepared for it and she had carried it out and she had not been sorry. She was not sorry now. She held her eyes open, watching the clock.

Not in this bed. She had sold the bed. The old-fashioned brass bedstead that he had hauled along into this apartment years ago. A sentimental touch. A prideful touch, an affectation. A rich man, but holding to simple tastes. A man of the people, the common people. Sleeping in an old-fashioned cheap bed. It gave him stature in his own eyes. Amid the splendor of his lot, and deep in his heart was that simplicity, that goodness. He had seemed to think it was a symbol of the pioneer, as though every wilderness cabin was fitted out with a brass bed. That had cleared his snob conscience so that he could sleep without knowing that everything he had was his at birth, and made him believe that he had come to eminence by the noble sweat of his brow. It seemed she had killed him for this, for this artificiality, this corruption, because his life had been in reality that of the ugliest parasitism and exploitation. She had thought a great deal about that afterward, recalling whole passages of Marxian doctrine, and knowing that she had struck a blow in behalf of the people . . . and for a few days she had believed it.

But then there had been another reason and it seemed truer. She had killed him because he was weak. She liked that reason because it seemed to make less sense. It defied the usual yardsticks of logic and motives. It had no recognition from the minds of the world. It defied all reasonable and orderly analysis. It was a motive only she could have had, only she could have understood.

It was false, too.

The real motive was commonplace. He had wanted a divorce. She did not know who the other woman was. She had made no effort to find out from him. She only knew that no one could cast her aside; no woman could usurp her place.

Two ropes had been necessary. Two nooses. The first to strangle him in the bed. She had prepared the other one beforehand. Then she had sat over him as he slept and put the first noose around his neck. She had passed the rope up and over the brass top of the head of the bed. She had got out of bed then, carrying the end of the rope with her out past the end of the bed, stood watching him from the foot of the bed as he slept with the noose still loose around his throat.

Nora flung off the covers, got out of bed, sharply awake, remembering. . . . She went to the closet and got a wool robe, and put it on, remembering Nanny, remembering the old woman's impudence, her threatening to leave for another job. Well, she would not leave. Not on her terms.

Yes, she had stood there for some time watching him sleeping unaware, with the noose around his neck, the rope leading up from his pillow between the close set vertical brass bars and over the top brass tube, then sloping down the length of the bed to her hands as she held the rope there, standing by the foot of the bed. She had realized the rope might bruise her palms and she'd gone to put on a pair of pigskin gloves. Then she'd gone back and taken the slack rope, and it had begun. . . .

The old woman would be sleeping soundly, or maybe not so soundly. It was a matter of indifference to Nora. She was the stronger of the two and if she had to subdue her with main force, she would do it. People did not walk out on Nora.

She remembered how she had grasped the rope in both gloved hands, looping it over the way she'd learned somewhere when helping handle ship's lines, so it wouldn't slip. Then she'd braced her feet, and the rope had come taut. She'd stepped back, pulling hard, and crouching and laying back so all her weight was on it. She'd felt it take hold. He had begun to thrash on the bed, and he made scraping sounds in his throat, and the bedclothes had begun to leap, as his legs kicked up under them, and his whole body had risen high like a hooked tarpon flying up and squirming in the air above the surface, then flopping again. She had watched his hand clawing around in between the upright brass posts, trying to get at the rope, trying to pull away, then trying to dig at it, but not hard, because there wasn't much fight left after just a little while. She thought maybe he'd been able to see her and understand it all, but she had never known. For a little while he'd slid upward, pushing with his hands and legs into the bed, rising to the top cross-rail of the head of the bed, his own head sliding up pressed between two of the uprights, too narrow

77

for him to get his head through. She'd had to move back fast when he pushed himself up that way so she could maintain the pressure, but it hadn't lasted too long. Still she'd waited, just leaning back holding the rope tight at arm's length for some time after he was quiet.

Then she'd put cushions beside the bed and put a blanket on top of them, and rolled him out onto the blanket so there wouldn't be any fall to bruise him. Then she's dragged him on the blanket into the bathroom, and got him propped sitting against the tub. She'd got her breath then, going out for awhile, and taking a cigarette and making the bed. But she'd not taken long because she wasn't sure about *rigor mortis*. When she got back in, she put on the gloves again, and started in on the hardest part of it.

Another rope with a noose was already in the bathroom. It was secured around the pipes under the wash basin. Then she had passed the noose up and across the steel shower curtain rod that ran lengthwise over the edge of the tub, and was embedded solidly in the wall. It was strong enough. The job then was to hoist him. She slung the rope which led from the noose he was in up and over the steel rod. Then she began to pull down. She never could have lifted him up, but she'd thought it wouldn't be too hard hoisting him that way. But it was hard. She'd broken out in sweat all over, and she had hung on the rope and it would budge and lift him an inch or so at a time. The sweat was running down from her hair into her eyes and ears and trickling down her body, and her arms were aching like fire and her shoulders felt as if they'd been stretched on a torture rack. To keep him from slipping back down she'd had to snub the rope under the edge of the wash basin, and wind it around the top of it and around the faucets while she stood and panted and tried to get up new energy. Inch at a time, inch up, hanging on, pulling and then hanging, shutting her eyes, her head swimming, her lungs aching from the strain, all of her wet and dripping sweat. It was

78

sliding down under her breasts and getting in her navel, and streaming down between her legs, so that her legs were wet clear to her feet, and the floor under her got slippery, so she had to get the rug. But finally he'd been high enough so his feet were off the floor several inches, just a few inches below the top of the tub.

Of course the police would have known in an instant, the way the rope was mashed, that he'd been pulled up. That was the reason for the other rope. She climbed up and stood with her bare feet curved over the edge of the tub, and got the free noose down around his neck, under the one he was hanging by. Then she got down again, loosened the rope that she'd just pulled him up by. His body fell the fraction of an inch and then the other noose had the weight, and she then got up and removed the first one. It was hard, not only standing there on the uncomfortable cold tub edge, but she didn't want to touch him more than she had to. She had to pull the noose wide enough to lift off, and it was messy, because the abrasive coil had cut the flesh. She was glad to be done with it. The rope he was in told its own story. It stretched with the fibers all pointing the way they should to prove to the police that the weight of his body had dropped into the noose, and the rope hadn't been used to hoist him. The original rope, with all its telltale mashed surfaces, she put carefully away in the bottom of a chest in the clothing vault back of the closet.

It had occurred to her to bathe, and she'd gone into the shower off his study and done it. Then she'd come back and got in bed, but she hadn't slept. She began to scream and to ring for the servants at seven.

Nanny had been among those who came. And now Nanny thought that she could leave without being bidden to leave. Nanny thought she could get Ed too on her side, could drive him away, keep him off as she had. . . .

Nora moved through the anteroom where her desk was, through his study, out into the hall, into the kitchen.

She pushed through the swing door into the dim-lighted hall of the servants' quarters, and stood a moment gazing at the doors, one after another. They were all closed. She went to Nanny's. She turned the knob silently and entered. She closed it behind her, then slipped the wool belt out of its loops in her robe. She hung the belt over her shoulder as she turned around and turned the door key.

CHAPTER VIII

NORA WALKED ON SOUNDLESS BARE feet straight ahead till she stood at the side of the bed. For several moments she looked down at the nearly motionless, irregular mound of bedclothes over the sleeping woman. She waited, listening to the slow, regular sound of breathing. Her eyes adjusted to the darkness. She pulled slowly at the belt on her shoulder, feeling the faint friction of wool on wool as it came down into her hand. She made a slipknot, looped it over her left wrist and pulled it hard, testing it with her right hand. She loosened the loop, pulled it wide till it formed a foot-wide circle.

She watched the sleeping woman. She was on her right side, faced away from Nora toward the window on the other side of the bed. Nora stepped to the right toward the head of the bed, bent down, peering closely at the woman's left cheek. She put out her fingers, touched the face lightly, then touched the eyelids. She withdrew her hand as the breathing tempo changed. The old woman stirred, snuffed twice, brought one hand up from under the covers and felt at her face, then began to turn over in the bed. Nora walked hurriedly, silently, to the foot of the bed.

For several seconds the room was filled with the heavy

dull squashing sounds of the mattress, of the several shiftings of the sleeping woman as she turned over, resettled herself, cleared her throat and swallowed, then sank again into slow, even breathing.

There was a four-foot space between the window wall and the bed. A big, overstuffed armchair stood back to the bed, faced toward the window. Beside it to the right was a narrow space, and then a table at the head of the bed on which stood a lamp, radio and clock. Nora sat on the arm of the chair peering toward the table, trying to make out the objects. Then, dropping the knotted belt back into the seat of the chair, she got down on her knees, felt out along the table legs till she located the lamp cord. She slid her fingers carefully down the cord and located the socket there in the wall just above the baseboard. She pulled out the lamp plug. She got up, sat again on the chair arm.

For awhile she watched the sleeping woman. Then she reached down, got the belt. She got to her feet. She stood a moment, sliding the belt in and out of the knot.

She put the belt in her pocket. She sat down, this time in the seat instead of on the arm of the chair. It must have been Nanny's favorite place. Looking out the window. Nora wondered what she looked at. The park? The apartments over on Central Park West? Maybe the sunsets. What if sometimes the old woman was sitting here while she was sitting or standing at the big front bedroom windows, looking at the same thing. At what? The slices of Hudson? The ships? The people on the walks and benches and lawns of the park? The people on the rowboat lake, the riders along the bridle path, the traffic? Or just at the sky? What would an old bitch look at, and what would she think about?

There were two, no three apartments lighted in the big Central Park West building straight across. In the one just north of it there wasn't any light. The next one had one, no, there was another, but was it the same building? No stars out. All clouds. Stuck away in a back room look-

81

ing at the same sights the mistress did . . . a young mistress . . . half, a third her age . . . well not a third, but about a two-and-a-half. Did she think there was any question who was who, who was boss and who wasn't? . . . did she maybe sit here and think she was really better? Did she think a lot about the fact Nora had been away to a sanitarium . . . did she like to think about that, think she didn't count, really, because her mind was diseased? Had she plotted to tell him, saved it up to tell him when he came? Did she think that no matter what Nora's position was she still didn't count; did she think Nora wasn't really boss?

Maybe she thought she could go away and spread tales to other people about her. Maybe she'd say to everyone, as she had to him, "Here's what she really is . . ." The old woman had talked to The Gray Eyes like that. She had got between her and hers. She had opened her mouth, she had made scornful remarks, she had told on her to The Gray Eyes.

But The Gray Eyes belonged to nobody else . . . to nobody else.

Nora stood up and took out the belt, and pressed to the side of the bed and said: "Old bitch." She doubled the belt, and switched the covers. She hit lightly, and the old woman didn't stir. Nora waited, listening; there was no break in the even breathing. She struck a little harder at the bulging covers over her hips. She hit again, and whispered: "That's one thing you can't do, come between us. . . . That was the last time you'll come between us . . . WAKE UP!" She said the last aloud, in a low, hoarse voice.

She stood rigid, tensed forward, the belt dangling from her clenched hand. "Wake up!" she whispered fiercely. The hissing sound seemed to hang there in the dark silence. She felt her heart begin to thump in quick, hard beats in her chest. There was no other sound. She poised, straining to listen. The old woman was not breathing.

"You're awake," she whispered.

There was no answer. There was the faintest shifting under the covers, then stillness.

"Admit it, you're awake!" Nora bent close, whispering almost soundlessly. "You are awake, you are breathing with your mouth open so you won't make any noise. If you make one sound I'll kill you!"

There was no answer.

Nora drew in a long breath, relaxed. She listened. The breathing continued, slow, regular as before. It hadn't stopped at all. The woman was asleep. She hadn't been awake. She backed away. The room seemed suddenly vast. A deep gray, high dim room. The red seemed large and far away and high. She spun about, stared at the square window, afraid suddenly that it was not a plain, small window, but three high, arched windows. She faced into the room again. It WAS large. It was HUGE. The windows back of her were tall and arched at the tops and in the bed a woman was sitting up and it was pitch black except for the light from the high windows, and the woman's face was dim, and it stared and stared, and its eyes were in deep black sockets. The woman was staring at her and Nora stayed still and motionless and crouching in the big room.

"Who is there?"

The voice came cold and ugly and threatening through the huge room.

"I see you."

She was small, and she was trapped motionless in front of the window, the top of her head just above the sill. She squatted down very slowly so her head wouldn't show.

"Nora, that is you! What are you doing in my room, you nasty little sneak. I'm coming to get you this minute and. . . ."

She's afraid, she's afraid, she's afraid, Nora thought. She's afraid to come. She's afraid of me.

"Nora, speak out. Tell me if it's you . . . tell me if you're in here . . . where are you . . . ?"

Nora stayed crouched, motionless. The figure on the bed lay down again. "Nightmares," it said. "Oh, God, these nightmares."

Nora waited, feeling her power over the old woman. The old woman was afraid, she told herself. Afraid to get out of the bed, afraid to move, afraid of her, afraid of her . . . waiting, waiting . . .

". . . it was only a nightmare," the woman said aloud into the dark.

She said it again, minutes later. After awhile she began to snore.

Suddenly Nora was cold and alone, the woman gone from her.

"NANNY!" Nora screamed. "NANNY . . . MRS. TRENT, wake up! Wake up! . . . hurry, wake up. Talk! It's you . . . it's you, Mrs. Trent . . ."

"What is it?" the old woman cried, waking, sitting up. "Who is it, what is it?"

"It's me . . . Mrs. Emlaine."

"You! What . . . what . . ."

"Don't turn on the lamp, Mrs. Trent. It's you . . . I'm in the right room . . ."

"It's me . . . what you want? . . . what you want in here? . . . You yelled, you woke me up. What you DOING standing there like that? . . . what you doing?"

"You were asleep . . . don't reach for the lamp—it's broke."

There was a noisy scramble, the hurried thumping of Mrs. Trent's feet hitting the floor. She ran to the door, snapped on the ceiling light at the wall switch.

"What you want? Get out of here. Don't look at me thataway . . . get out."

"Don't be frightened. I tried to wake you . . . Mrs. Trent, you mustn't leave me . . ."

"I wouldn't stay for a million dollars. I got me a good job, I wouldn't stay here for a million dollars. You get out of here . . . you go on, now . . ."

She swung and grabbed and twisted the doorknob and

pulled. "It won't open . . . IT WON'T OPEN!" She started to scream. Nora swung into motion, caught the end of the bed, swung herself around it, catapulted herself toward the old woman, her hands extended. She grabbed her shoulders, dug her fingers into the flesh under the cotton nightgown, spun her around.

"Don't yell, you damned fool. It's locked. Get away, I'll open it."

"I'll yell if I want—you're crazy . . ." Her voice pitched high, hysterical . . . as if the full impact of the situation had just struck. She stared wide-eyed, mouth open . . . pulled back. "Get out quick, get out quick, get out quick . . . look at you . . . get away from me . . . don't come near me . . . don't touch me. Look at your face. Why'd you come here in the middle of the night? Why'd you come into my room in the dark like that? You crazy woman, you . . . you crazy woman, get out . . . oh, you get out of here . . ."

"Nanny . . . I mean, Mrs. Trent . . ."

"Fasten your robe, you shameless naked crazy woman . . . I never want to look at your shameless body again . . . I never do. There's something terrible about you . . . something awful about you . . . don't come shameless naked with yourself around me ever . . . I seen you . . . more'n once I seen you . . . the way you feel yourself up and down, the way you do yourself like something shameless, like loving your ownself, you filthy shameless bitch. Git git git . . . quick, quick . . . I'll bash you . . . I'll bash you, woman. . . ."

"Please, Mrs. Trent. Will you listen? Will you please listen? Will you listen? Will you stop talking and listen? Don't leave me. You'll never have to come near me. You won't be my maid. Just housework. You mustn't leave. You mustn't go to a new place. I'll pay extra . . . listen to me . . . listen to me . . . I'll make you a present . . . a thousand dollars. You mustn't go . . . a thousand dollars. . . ."

"Not for a million, I said . . . no, never."

"You don't believe it, but you'd never have to serve me. You'd just work at housework. Clyde would be who you worked for . . . I'll write it out . . . I'll write out a check now . . . come with me and I'll write out a promise about the kind of work you do. You'll never have to serve me at all. I'll write it out . . . and the check I'll write . . . right now . . ."

"You'd really do it?" The doubt was still strong in her voice.

"I promise."

"Well . . ." The muscles in Mrs. Trent's face worked at the problem. With a thousand dollars—savings, security—she could always up and walk out if later Nora tried to back down on her promise. Besides, with the promise written down maybe it would work out all right. Then she wouldn't have to move, accustom herself to new ways. She looked around the little room, feeling it home after so many years.

Nora waited as the woman put on slippers, a robe. She unlocked the door. They went into the hall. The butler, Clyde, was standing outside the door in robe and slippers.

"Mrs. Trent was upset. She was thinking of leaving. I've persuaded her it's best to stay. She has made her home here." Her direct gaze challenged him to question her. "I am giving her an agreement that she needn't take orders direct from me." Nora stopped, drew her robe closed as she detected the direction of the butler's fixed downward stare. He looked up, met her eyes guiltily. She pulled the belt from her pocket by one end. The noose end dropped to the floor. Nora smiled, caught it up, unwrapped the belt and tied it around her waist. "It would be a terrible thing for her to go out into a strange place after all these years. Isn't that so, Clyde?"

He nodded.

"You must all realize that I haven't been myself or—or she wouldn't have thought of leaving. Would you, Mrs.

Trent?" Nora said. "It's only since—since I've been alone that I was mean—you know that."

Mrs. Trent tipped her head, thoughtfully. "Now I think of it, it's the truth."

Nora sat at the small desk in the room adjoining her bedroom, and wrote:

"Mrs. Trent will henceforth receive her orders only from Clyde. Signed, Nora Emlaine."

Mrs. Trent held the slip of paper in her hand, the hope in her face vanquishing the doubt. "I'll have to call up the other people and tell them I won't be coming there," she said.

"You should, Mrs. Trent," Nora said, friendly. "You can do it in the morning." Then she wrote out a check for one thousand dollars. Handing it to her, Nora said:

"Just remember sometimes that the late Mr. Emlaine didn't think of any of you in his will."

When Nora woke late the next morning she felt worn but at peace. She sent for Clyde.

"How is Mrs. Trent?"

"Just fine, Mrs. Emlaine. It was a very decent thing you did."

"Thanks, Clyde. I hope you won't think she is the only one to get a present."

"Oh, Mrs. Emlaine!"

"No indeed . . . Did she call and say she couldn't take the job?"

"Yes, ma'am."

"Did she cash the check yet? Deposit it?"

"I don't believe so. I know she hasn't, I mean."

"Good. Listen, Clyde. She takes her orders from you now, of course."

"She showed me the note."

"You take yours from me, however. Send her in. I'm ready for my bath."

"But, Mrs. Emlaine . . ."

"That's all, Clyde."

"But, Mrs. Emlaine, I don't think Mrs. Trent will . . ."

"Oh, we'll have to chance that. She *did* notify them she wasn't taking the other job."

"Yes, but Mrs. Emlaine . . ."

"Before you go, set the phone over here by the bed and plug it in."

He did so, moving reluctantly, shaking his head.

"I'm afraid," he began, "that I can't accept your order. I'll send another maid for your personal service."

Nora dialed, not looking at him.

"Do as you please, Clyde," Nora said, smiling briefly. "That will be all."

A girl's voice came over the phone. "Depositors Trust, good morning."

"Mr. Greedon, please," Nora said. ". . . . this is Nora Emlaine . . . yes . . . thank you, just fine. I'm sorry to trouble you, Mr. Greedon, but I am afraid I did something terribly thoughtless, and it must be remedied. I wrote a check for a thousand dollars to a Mrs. Margaret Trent . . . it was all a misunderstanding, and I want payment stopped. . . . Yes . . . yes . . . no, it hasn't been presented for payment. I know that . . . yes, thank you so much. . . ."

Nora waited for a maid. One of the younger ones came. "Wipe the frown off your face and get a little snap in your tail. . . ."

The girl turned around, wordless, and left the room. Nora laughed. "Pack and get out!" Nora called.

"Don't you ever worry on that score, don't you ever let it worry that dizzy smelly head of yours, MA'AM."

"Tell Clyde the same goes for him . . . likewise that other young snip . . ."

There was no answer. By the middle of the afternoon they had all gone.

"Now!" she thought. "Now!"

She felt exuberant. There was nothing left of the old

world. A stray scattering of old friends sometimes telephoned, but they would be simply disposed of. She had never realized that this was what she wanted. She was happy. Happy. Happy.

She telephoned 5-A Ads.

"I want Ed Harlon."

"He's not at this office."

"It's very important."

"He talk to you about an ad?"

"Yes. He talked to me. He wanted me to give him my decision."

"You can reach him at——"

She scribbled the number.

CHAPTER IX

ED HAD KNOWN SHE WOULD CALL AND that he'd be going back. And he did go back, often, in the weeks that followed. Mostly to her place, but occasionally to restaurants where she would sign the check. When he protested she'd shrug it off and look at him so sweetly that he'd feel squelched and would leave a tip bigger than anything he'd ever spent on whole dinners for himself and Edna. He never knew just how to act with her. She said she wanted him to be the boss; then she'd get in a bossy mood and start throwing her weight around. He'd tell her off, scared every time he did it that she'd throw him out. Sometimes she took it sweet as an angel, and would give him one of those melting, good-little-girl gazes that turned him inside out. At other times she'd stomp off and lock herself in the bedroom. Nothing would bring her out. He'd finally leave, half-hoping it was for good. But the next day at 5-A he wouldn't be able to work. All he could put his mind to was Nora . . . and would she call? . . . wouldn't she call? . . . now she's getting out of bed . . . now she's dressing . . . no, showering . . . then dressing, no, being dressed . . . maids helping her. What a sweet job that would be, getting that gorgeous, under-glass piece of stuff into her scanties.

Then the call would come, and that doll voice would be in his ear. "Ed, I was bad. I'm sorry . . . will you give me another chance? . . ." Would he! He'd give her his arms, his legs, his heart and head and lungs and liver. Damn, it was true, she'd created him. When he was with her he was living . . . when he was away from her he was dead. The look of her, the smell of her, the touch of her . . .

He started knocking 'em dead on the phone at 5-A. Grim, he'd barrel into his spiels, thinking, *for you, baby, for you*. He had to make it, now. This was it. He knew where he was going. Right up into her league. Knock 'em dead. Hang on. Don't let the sucker slip off the line. Every buck counted. Everything focused on Nora. It didn't happen, a girl like Nora . . . not once in a century. A guy didn't get that kind of a break except maybe from Fate. You made good on it. You got up to her where you could say, baby, you want this? you want that? It's yours. Me to you. Forget that dough your husband left you. Baby, you're mine.

The only hell of it was if he got grim over the phone it hurt his spiel. A pitch had to roll, easy and strong and confident. Once the sucker felt you were panting, it was NG. His sales didn't pick up. Far from it, just to be frank with himself. Sometimes he had to draw eating money. Other times he blew in too much on some present for her. It was nuts, just nuts to blow it on cheap stuff when she could get anything, and the top quality, by just using one of her charge accounts. But he couldn't stop himself. The way she'd act when she got a little present would just wilt him down. Like a baby, like a beautiful, beautiful baby. You'd think it was a million bucks he was laying at her feet . . . and that's just where he'd lay it too, by God, if he had it . . . WHEN he had it. Think big, and bang, suddenly there'd be a proposition ready-made, and he'd swoop in on it and *click*. He'd be up there. That's how love did. It made you smart and tough. Exactly how he'd click . . . well, the details, that's strictly subordinate stuff. Big-time thinkers left the details to the help. Toss 'em a few grand bonuses, etc., etc.

F'r instance, what he should sharp up on was the horses. Patience, then wham! A killing. Watch for the right time, the right race. Maybe no play for days, weeks. He could hold tight, play it like a poker hand. Then wham it in on the nose, five or ten grand . . . and say 100-to-1. Then maybe invest the capital, just for a cushion in case . . .

Then he'd stroll in on her and just for a gag he'd have one of those clown 1-foot cigars in his kisser just to make her giggle, then he'd say: "Emlaine . . . I don't like that name." Like she'd said about his name that time at the Central Park Zoo. "Emlaine . . . I'm willing to take that name off your hands at a discount. . . ." He'd better write the thing out, and sling in some big business and high finance words to show he wasn't just bulling but was solid big league. "Well, Ed, I do not know," she would say. He would say: "I know. That will suffice." Kindly, but masterful, so she would know there'd be no more nonsense and bitchiness and abusing the hired help, like she did that poor old lady.

That bitchiness wasn't Nora. It was just something that came over her. Or maybe just a showing off, like some little kids. They'd knock themselves out to get attention. Do anything. The point was Nora was special and she had to have attention. His attention! And after all, when she was nasty, she got sorry, as if she knew it was wrong and wanted to be right. And she was, deep down underneath. Right.

Well, maybe she had been to a sanitarium. But what the hell. All the rich dames ducked out when things got

tough . . . or what *they* thought was tough. They should
know what he'd been through if they wanted to know
what tough was. Still, Nora wasn't like any other rich
dame, or any dame in the universe, and she'd probably
had to get away from that husband of hers. Imagine, the
poor girl trying to live with a guy who was always
threatening to commit suicide. Why, a thing like that was
criminal to do to a sensitive, artistic type girl like her. It
wasn't that she wasn't good enough; she was too good.
The bug docs, just like she said, didn't understand anybody as special as her.

He, Ed Harlon, was no bug doctor, but one thing he'd
say. He knew Nora. So, she changed her moods like she
did her dresses. Mean and sweet and silly and dignified
and childish and sophisticated . . . she ran through all
the parts from a baby with tantrums to an imperious
old dowager. Better than a hundred actresses put together. So, if she went nearly off her rocker on account
of the husband she'd had, still she hadn't gone clear off!

With the right kind of a husband, one that understood
her and made her feel easy the way she said he did . . .
Well, even if he hadn't quite made his fortune, he intended to, didn't he? Sure he did. He was sincere. Never,
absolutely never, would he let any woman keep him.

Still, he let himself imagine what it might be like if he
was in . . . really in solid. One thing he knew, he didn't
want this just to be a hit and run affair. Maybe it was
even better that he hadn't got to bed with her . . . Solid
and permanent, like the view from her apartment window . . . like the Chase National Bank. No! he didn't
mean to think like that. Christ, he loved her, didn't he?
Sure he did. She was driving him nuts, wasn't she? Still,
he wondered how much dough she really had. All he
could think of was plenty. It must've cost her three grand
a month just to live as she did . . . That was probably
just skimming off a part of the interest on the capital.
Three G's a month just for bed and board, practically.
Why that was more than he made in a day. He grinned.

That was witty, he'd have to spring it on her . . . casual, of course, not like he was interested in her dough . . .

Any mention of money made her swing off into that stuff about The Gray Eyes and how she had created him and them. But, what the hell, what she wanted was his gray eyes always to be looking at her, naked and beautiful. There were worse propositions than that. It didn't mean she was off her rocker. It was just her way of saying she went for him.

Ed wasn't prepared for the switch she pulled on him. It was in her apartment. She was lying on the mile-long leather affair under the weird painting of the city under the ocean. She was on her back, arms under her head, staring up and babbling away about something childish or other. Suddenly she was on her feet. Her moods changed fast, but this one was like lightning. She stood there, clear-eyed, down-to-earth and looked at him calmly. He began to feel a little self-conscious, sitting there like a sot, sipping whisky. He got to his feet, sensing something big. She said quietly:

"Will you marry me?"

"Marry you?" he repeated stupidly.

"Yes. Will you marry me?"

"You really mean that?"

She shrugged impatiently. "Of course I mean it. Will you marry me?"

"Right away, you mean?"

"Yes. As soon as we can. I want to get away."

He started to finish off his drink. He shook his head, set it down. This was it, wasn't it? The dream, coming true . . . only not quite *his* dream. He had a funny feeling . . . it wasn't exactly his dream, just *like* his dream, and that he wasn't making it happen, it was being done *to* him somehow.

"You're rich," he said.

"Is there anything wrong with that?"

"Well . . . it's only that I'm not a . . . I mean, you don't think I'd let a woman keep me?"

"I could keep you very well."

"Look." He cleared his throat, stood firmer. "I'm not much maybe, yet. But nobody could ever say Ed Harlon would let a woman keep him."

"You've got pride?" she asked.

"Yes," he said, feeling hurt.

"An all-American boy. Your hero is Fearless Fosdick."

"Laugh. OK. Laugh. I still say, maybe I'm not perfect, but . . ."

"Will you marry me, Ed?"

"Not like this . . ." He gestured futilely. She would not let things get in the right key. She kept pushing it, throwing him off balance. "Christ, I'd love to marry you . . ."

"Then will you?"

He glanced sharply at her, hearing the new note in her voice, one that was almost wheedling.

"Yes, Nora. When I can support you."

"I'll be waiting in my wheelchair."

"Have your gags."

"But I can support you, Ed. That's the point."

"I won't marry you right away."

"Then leave me with my broken heart," she mocked. "Good-by, good-by."

"Nora, you know I love you."

"Do you, Ed?"

"Yes. Yes, I love you. I love you very much."

"Then I'll be waiting in my wheelchair when you round the bend of the road to the old folks' home. When you've made your fortune."

"Don't make fun of me."

"Don't shout in my hearing-aid when you come."

"I won't." He didn't know for sure yet what she was doing but he was beginning to see his part. "This is harder on me than on you. I really love you, Nora."

"Love conquers all. Love conquers pride. Listen, if you've got a flag, let's wave it and sing the national anthem, then a rousing chorus of 'Good-by Forever.'"

"Don't you ever stay serious? Don't you believe in anything?"

"Serious? I'm weeping. Wave Old Glory, Ed."

"I love you."

"I know," she said, her artificial gaiety replaced by a mock seriousness. "And now you're about to make the big sacrifice of your honor."

"I don't get it."

"Come on, Ed." Was she getting impatient? "You've got yourself convinced that it'll be all right marrying me in spite of my money because you love me."

"I do love you."

"Then you're ready to sacrifice yourself?"

"Aw, Nora." He felt pushed around, pushed in the right direction but pushed. "You don't think I'd *like* living on your money?"

"I think you'd love it," she said.

"Well if that's what you think . . ."

"Just between us, it's true."

He didn't say anything, knowing this was the crucial moment, figuring his move.

"I can't see what you'd want of me . . . what I have to offer."

"I know," she said, and now he knew her impatience was real. "Come off it, Ed. Haven't we pulled all the stops? I hate lying talk."

He drew in his breath. He wasn't quite able to look at her. "I'd have to have something in my own name. I couldn't come asking for a fifty or a hundred every time I needed it."

"It's a deal."

"Fifty thousand?" he kept his voice firm.

"Five."

"Fifty."

"No," Nora said, and the tone of her voice told him they were nearing the end of the act. "You'll have no living expenses. Five."

"I'll need clothes, a car . . ."

"Full wardrobe, a car, plus five."

This, he knew, was it. He couldn't help trying to get them back on the proper level. "If I didn't love you I wouldn't think of it."

"We passed that phase," she said, and then, shortly: "I'm very tired, Ed. Let's call it a night, and a deal."

He was tired, too. Later, alone, he realized just how tired. His feelings were a curious mixture. There was a glow of achievement but it was faint. Which was foolish because he had gotten what he wanted. Or nearly. And there was the feeling too that he had been had. It was a feeling he knew would pass.

CHAPTER X

THERE WERE, ED FELT NOW, DRIVING south with Nora, only a couple of flies in the ointment. First, there was no snow to leave. There should have been snow. Second, it was too cold to lower the top of his new car. But, pulling out of Charleston, he lowered it anyway. Then they rode toward Florida in the proper style. He tried to think if he had any other troubles. He felt practically giddy, sort of unanchored without them. There were none. He had sixty dollars worth of leather on his feet. Sixty. Not six. Not sixteen. Sixty. "What I want on my hoofs is a 25-buck set of shoes," he had said. But she knew where to get them for a hundred, two hundred. For him, that was too much . . . well, maybe that troubled him too, he thought, feeling comical as hell. Wearing only sixty-buck shoes when they had two hundred-buck ones.

In Richmond he began to say "you-all" and "suh." Taking the roller-coaster highway through Virginia and spotting the historical markers he began to point out one side, then the other. "That's Valley Forge," he said. "Look, quick—see that? That's Valley Forge." Everything was Valley Forge. "Nora, look, quick, what's that? —guess—" "Washington Monument?" "Nope." "Europe?" "Almost." "It's Remember the Alamo." "Nope. Valley Forge." "No-o-o-o!" "Yes! Aw-aw, there's another marker—did you see what it was, Nora?" "Valley Forge." "Right!"

Red leather cushions. Maroon body. A hood a mile long with a naked chrome dame out in front cutting the wind apart for them. Sixteen cylinders. One great big long purr of power that was pure music. He'd jam the gas just to feel that purr get down and growl and pull his belly back through the seat. You didn't drive a new car ninety. Now did you? Was it sensible? Sure you didn't—so he did.

"Look—my eyes closed, no hands," he'd yell at her, and she'd yelp and sit bolt upright out of her doze, and he'd bray with laughter, feeling it spill back of him in the wind. "I thought that'd make you wake up and look over at me."

"I don't have to look," she'd say. "You're in my dreams too."

What were you going to do with a dame like that? Love her to hell and gone. Then come back and start over.

"They broke the pattern when they made you," he said. "They got discouraged. They never could repeat. You know that, don't you?"

She would smile at him; she'd give him that delicious sweet-eyed little girl look, happy, wonderful, beautiful. This was living. This was what fate was saving up for him all along. She was his. A cynical part of his mind nudged him with the thought that she and all that dough were his, his till death did them part. But he didn't listen to that. He felt good so he was good. He was above pettiness and meanness. He chased away a fantasy of piles of hundred dollar bills and flashed her a glance of warm affection. That was the real him, he told himself. That was the way he really felt. Then they were in Miami Beach, and he bent the bus around a moon-shaped driveway up to the entrance of a sky-high scrubbed white hotel on Collins, and began to shuck off buck tips from a big wad, and strolled into the red and blue flagstoned lobby with his lady and a retinue of bellboys, showing the reservation verification and scuffing their names indolently on the desk card: "Mr. and Mrs. Edward Harlon, New York City." He scanned the scenery of gold and bronze and beet and milk-colored flesh lounging and moving out beyond the terrace on the white sand, and remarked in the elevator with detachment that the ocean seemed to be in the same old place.

There was a week of unusual, which was to say good, weather and his body pinked and then browned a little, and he grew more and more in his sense of power and joy, slipping easily into the life of idle plenty such as he had always dreamed of. He was up by ten, to race out into the water and swim himself limp, and then to shower and dress and find Nora having fruit juice and coffee on the street-side terrace. She would be delighted to see him and she would look fresh and pretty in a big hat and candy colored or white cotton dress. Sometimes she sat in halter and shorts on a deck chair, looking out over the water, silent, and when he would come in spluttering and laughing and breathing hard at well earned breath she would smile at him so tenderly that he'd flop down in the sand and hold her hand and love her with moonsick calf eyes, and try to think of something different and special he could buy for her, or do for her.

He had flowers sent up, and candy, and a big creamy panda, and a huge wool dog and sometimes he drove over to Lincoln Road and parked, and then he'd walk along the pink sidewalks window shopping the swanky shops and buy a playsuit or some kind of fancy-fancy clogs or sandals or bracelets or sets of earrings and necklaces made out of colored shells or coral—or maybe he'd buy her a hat that would seem dizzy on any other girl in the world. Compacts, cigarette lighter and case, jeweled sunglasses, once a necklace and earring set that cost seven hundred and fifty. She had all sorts of gowns, or he'd have surely bought one certain Grecian sort with one bare shoulder that would have been perfect on her. He couldn't resist a set of black lace things—bra, panties and short slip. She had plenty of stuff like that, and they cost him over two hundred, but when he went back to the hotel and she went right up and put them on for him, delighted and happy and giggling, he didn't mind the price.

After breakfast they'd drive over for a batch of different tipsheets and the racing form, then drive around, going over the causeway into Miami, then go to Hialeah. He bet them fifty a throw "On the Nose." That was his way. Right on the nose. Whatever he'd bet she'd take the same horse. Once he remembered collecting six hundred on one race, and she collected the same. In a week he dropped over a thousand.

They went to the Jai Alai, and stuffed on Cuban sandwiches between games, and yelled their heads off and not a night passed they didn't collect on a Quiniella, and once they hit the daily doubles. They never got to the dog races because they kept winning at Jai Alai. He'd take a double shot at the bar between games if he collected, a single if he lost, and on the last game he'd always have hunches and play heavy, and Nora followed his choices exactly, and somehow the last game would land them back to earth and maybe they'd be five or ten bucks ahead, not subtracting the prices of drinks and sandwiches and admission price.

No races on Sunday, no Jai Alai, and he swam too much, and the brightness of the sand and water depressed him a little. Nora sat on a deck chair sunning herself and staring out over the water through sunglasses, and seemed scarcely to notice him when he came and sprawled beside her. He remembered he got

99

interested in a foursome giggling and cavorting down by the water edge, tossing a beach ball; sometimes one of the guys, instead of throwing it over the girls to the other man, would bounce it off the rump of a cute little blonde dancy thing in white shorts and halter. He was thinking he'd like to play around with that, and it was good thinking. It had been lonely, only him and Nora. They had talked with no one. Then he realized that Nora was looking at the side of his face. He turned and grinned at her:

"Those guys must live in the sun," he said. "Wish I was tanned like that."

"You're not interested in their tans," she said. It was a statement neither angry nor playful, but it wiped the grin from his face. She stared through the dark lenses, her face composed, expressionless. "You're getting broke, aren't you?"

"No."

"You haven't two thousand."

"Oh, yes I have."

"Remember the hotel is a hundred a day."

"I remember," he said impatiently.

"Tomorrow I will phone a real estate agent," she said. "We'll get a house somewhere on the shore."

"Why," he asked irritably. "Why should we do that?"

"Because I want to. I'm not going back to New York." Her voice was coldly firm, unpleasantly decisive. "We have to live somewhere. I don't like hotels." The girl pursued the ball past them. "People, people, people," Nora said, and suddenly her voice became persuasively warm. "I want you alone. You know that."

But he did not like it. "I thought you were having a swell time."

"It's all right."

"I thought we'd go back to New York then."

"No. I wired to sublet the apartment. I'm never going back there."

"You mean we'd live here in Miami?"

"Somewhere in the county, probably . . . or in the next county, some county. Something off to itself, on the ocean . . ."

"I've got to be thinking about getting back to work. . . ."

She laughed, and he didn't like it. He didn't like the thought that she was keeping him. More, he didn't like the thought that she might be feeling she was keeping him, could control him.

"It's not funny. Not 5-A. But I've got to do something. I might invest in something, or . . . well, look here, you have got connections, investments in some damned big concerns."

"Well?"

"Well, you could give me introductions, suggest . . ."

"I don't know anything about the business. It's all handled through the executors. Besides, you don't need to work."

"It gets hot here pretty soon . . . we won't want to stay here . . . we could go see your lawyers and see if there isn't a spot someplace. You know I know advertising. If I was in an organization that . . ."

"I don't know anything about it. We're staying in Florida," she said.

"Listen, Nora. Be reasonable. I have to have some sort of occupation."

"You think there's some virtue in work?"

"No, but——" He didn't. But stubbornly he knew that he needed to have a job, needed it for his—his "independence." That girl . . . just because he'd looked . . . Surprised at the intrusion of a thought he had not known he had, he flashed a glance at Nora. He wondered if she could be jealous. He liked the thought. But he didn't like the way she had reacted if that was it.

"I've got to do things, so we can feel right about each other, you know what I mean? I got to be somebody of some kind . . ." he said. "So you'd keep your respect for me."

"You care what I think?"

"Of course I do."

She laughed quietly.

"I really mean it—all right, so you're thinking I took the car and clothes and the money so it means I'm cheap . . ."

"Let's not start in on honor again."

"I'm going in for a drink," he said.

They didn't talk about it any more. When they were ready to go out for dinner she was her old self again. And better. She was more provocatively lovely than he'd ever seen her. Her hair was upswept. Her skin was like rich cream. She wore a silver lamé gown sheathed tight across her hips and thighs, falling to the instep and slit halfway, to the knee. Her feet in a lacework of silver-strap sandals were bare and brown, with deep red polish on the nails. Her back, arms, sides, shoulders and the rich swelling pale upper slopes of her breasts were bare. She came near him and there was a tantalizing scent of perfume rising warm and delicious from her body. Her face was unrouged, but her lips were full and vivid under heavy lipstick. Her brows were arched finely, the lashes very black, the upper lids blue shadowed. She stood with her hands lightly on the shoulders of his white dinner jacket and swayed her shoulders slowly and looked at him with an odd, secretive smile. Without seeming to have moved at all she was against him, her body pressing with subtle warmth, and then she had stepped back a few inches, but her hands remained, and she smiled devilishly.

"No!" she whispered, shrugging as he touched her bare shoulder.

She was pressed close to him again, and he gripped her to him, his hands low on her back, partly on the lamé, partly on her warm skin. He pulled her body in tight against him, and she raised her lips. They were a little apart and smiling, and her eyelids were lowered nearly shut, and she whispered:

"I'm all made up . . . we mustn't spoil it."

But she waited, her face lifted, her body yielding to him, and she was so beautiful he ached. He couldn't resist. He raised his hands to the smooth, lovely upper part of her back and pulled her close, and lowered his mouth, feeling the slight yielding of her lips under the pressure of his, tasting the pleasant flavor of the lipstick, feeling the warmth of her mouth. And then she kissed him. It was really the first time. He knew it was the first time when it began. He hadn't known before how much she had withheld.

Her arms slid around him and locked tight. He could feel her knees and thighs and the small bowing of her stomach and her breasts. Her lips moved as though she were talking rapidly and articulating every sound. They hardened and relaxed, and clinging to his, were alive and hot. She held on, and she clenched tighter with her arms, then relaxed one arm and ran her fingers along his cheek and over his ear and on his neck. She mashed herself to him and made a small whimpering sound low in her throat, and when, breathless, he drew his head back, she cupped the back of his head in both hands and held on, keeping her lips to his, working them.

He stood panting and trembling, looking at her smeared mouth as she stared, her eyes glazed. She clasped his face suddenly between her hands again and kissed him, drawing away, then pressing her lips hard, drawing back, pressing again.

He bent and began to kiss her neck and her shoulders and then her breasts. She pulled back. He caught her arms and kissed them, and kissed her hands, and then her throat again. "I love you, darling," he whispered. "I love you, love you . . . let's not go out yet, darling. God, you're so beautiful . . . I want to love you . . . all of you, I have to have you, darling . . ."

"Darling . . ." she said.

He was never to forget it. It occurred once. She had responded as never before or again. She had known how

103

to love and to be loved and he remembered it over and over later, almost incredulous at himself, at her, at the unplanned perfection, the abandonment. Afterward, it was clear to him. All of it came back in full, exquisite detail as though between them they'd achieved a sort of wonderful delirium. "But they broke the pattern after they made it that evening," he would think. Maybe the look she'd seen him give that girl . . . but that was silly.

Sometimes he'd wish it hadn't happened. If he'd never known what he was missing, the rest wouldn't be so hard to take. He'd never have recognized that she was unsatisfactory to love, that she was lifeless, unresponsive to his greatest efforts. Maybe he could have kept on imagining that she was as wonderful as her loveliness promised. Maybe he'd have managed to go on thinking he only imagined that she was disappointing.

Throughout the rest of that night, after they had finally gone to dinner, then to a night club, and finally out to a casino to play roulette he had had a feeling of contentment, a restful feeling of closeness with her. They had moved through the long evening with very little to say to each other. When he had spoken or when they had danced together he had been full of tenderness. She had seemed to him to be of the same mood. In fact she had been in no mood at all, but very nearly blank, saying nothing, watching the show with faint interest, watching him drink without any particular feeling about him or what they were doing. She played roulette like an automaton, laying her chips on zero and double zero at each spin, losing steadily, disinterestedly. People had watched her, and it had seemed to Ed that they thought she looked like a painting or a statue—so beautiful you couldn't believe it.

Later, he thought back and wondered if they thought she was doped or dead drunk, the way she'd sat there emotionless and unaware of everything, just shoving chips out automatically, having him buy more, playing zero and double zero over and over. Winning four times, doubling up her bets, losing them all, having him buy more, losing finally over eight hundred dollars.

That episode, though he didn't know it then, marked a turning point in their life. It was as if the climax of their loving had been not merely the climax of that act, but of all that had gone before. Thereafter he found himself unable to reach her physically or emotionally, more and more bewildered by her moods and mercurial changes.

When he woke, late in the morning Monday, she was gone and there was a note that she would be out the whole day with the real estate men. He stood staring at the water and the beach fourteen floors below and did not go swimming. He totaled his check stubs—once again. There was not more than a few hundred above the hotel bill. He didn't leave the room. He sent down for a bottle and some magazines, then propped his feet on the sill and looking out on the ocean, drank and dozed off, reading, drinking, smoking, dozing. When he woke late in the afternoon, he heard the sizzing of the shower and went in and found her there.

"Why'ncha wake me up and kiss me," he said, starting to take off his clothes.

"I found a place," she said. "It's wonderful. Don't take off your clothes."

"I need a shower," he said. "That's what I need. Not a wonderful place that my wife goes out and leases without a how-you-like-it or go-to-hell."

"Don't take your clothes off till I'm done."

"I want to," he said. "I want you, darling. I want you close, naked with me, darling. I want to touch you. Just feel you, be close to you, close as two people can get . . ."

He stood stripped and watched her, standing lathering, the water splashing on her bathing cap, streams of it rolling glisteningly over her shoulders, zigzagging down her body, over and around her breasts. They were

105

very white because her shoulders and midriff were tanned. Her hips and lower stomach were sharply white too, against the line of tan curving up high around her thighs. She looked like she was in a pair of white shorts. He stepped toward the tub.

"Don't get in," she said. She lifted a knee, soaped it with a big spongy cloth.

"Sure I'll get in," he said. "I can't keep away. Jeez, no matter what you do, Nora . . . renting a place like that, not thinking of what I want, or . . ."

She stood up straight. "You can get the hell out of my life altogether if you choose. You're not chained."

"Aw, darling . . ." he grinned, and stepped over the tub edge.

"I told you not to get in here," she said.

She lifted her forearm across her body, the soapy cloth dangling down over one breast. "Get out," she said.

He grinned, watched the water pouring across her shoulder, down along her arm so that it looked polished.

"Anybody tell you you had a pretty elbow?" he said. "Anybody ever kiss you there?" He bent toward her—her arm whipped out, the washcloth slapped him across the mouth.

"No," she said coldly. "Nobody ever did."

"Well, is that a nice thing to do? God damn it, I ask you is that a nice thing to do?—here, let me get a handful of water and get the soap out of my mouth . . ."

She lifted the cloth back over her shoulder, and swung it forward viciously so it smacked lengthwise into his face, hitting his hair and forehead and nose. "I told you to get out . . . now do it . . ."

"I'm God damned if I will."

"Then I'll get out and wait for you, you filthy animal. I'll be waiting in the other room till you finish . . ."

"All RIGHT, I'll leave," he said. He went out and had a long shot out of the whisky bottle. He had a second one, and then thought: "Oh, what's the percentage in staying mad." She came out and dressed, composedly.

"I'm starved," he said good-humoredly.

"I am too. Can you still afford to buy dinner for us?"

"Hell, yes."

"Keep enough for the hotel bill."

"Don't let it bother you."

"Tomorrow, we'll spend the day laying in provisions and I've got some cleaning people readying things, so we'll be able to check out of here tomorrow."

"Honeymoon's over . . . *you're* ending it, that it?"

"I've got a lot on my mind. I want to be alone, you understand. I want to get off alone."

"Does that include me?"

"Of course it does . . . you're part of me."

"Wait a second, Nora. Are we back on the—on the—you know—did you create me, Nora? Tell me."

"I wonder, Ed. I've wondered a lot about it since last night . . ."

"Since—since before we went out? Since that?"

She nodded, got out her lipstick brush, turned away from him to the mirror. He shrugged, went into the shower. Nora turned her head an inch to one side and stood with the lipstick brush poised in mid-air and looked into the mirror out of the corner of her eyes. Standing across the floor by the wall, staring at her with one eye around the side of her upper arm was the black wool dog. She swayed her body sidewise until she could see the other eye and the rest of the dog's head beside her arm in the mirror.

Cautiously, she laid the lipstick brush on the dresser top. She turned around, pretending to be interested in something within the open closet on the other side of the room. She walked a step, slid her glance at the dog waiting and watching there from the floor, saw that the dog was unaware that she wasn't really going to the closet. She took another step toward the closet, then altering her course with swift unexpectedness, ran directly and quietly to the dog, bent, swooped it up.

Spinning, she carried it to the window. She hurled it out.

She leaned out, braced on the sill, watching the creature hurtle. He glanced off the edge of a big beach umbrella, then struck the sand. A figure appeared from beneath the umbrella, and another man and a girl walked across the sand and looked down at the dog, then up. Nora withdrew into the room, went back to her mirror, and took up her lipstick brush with a relieved sigh.

PART TWO

CHAPTER I

IT TOOK ONLY A FEW DAYS FOR ED HARLON to adjust to his new role as master of a seaside estate. In the near isolation he quickly came to feel the same expansiveness he'd got the first time he went to the big Emlaine apartment. He would stroll about the secluded grounds in slacks and sport shirt, pausing to inspect some feature or other with a sober air of proprietorship, and send his gaze in a calm survey of the grounds and house from various points. Morning and afternoon and evening he would set out on a sort of tour of inspection, moving with extreme leisure, with a vague notion that it was the occupation of squires, that without proper surveillance the trees might grow too fast or too slowly. He maintained a sort of vigilance, half sensing that in this way order would prevail.

Or, maybe he thought he was establishing himself, displaying a to-the-manor-born nature. He hoped to fit into the setting. It was the basic difference between him and Nora. Whatever the setting, she tried to fit it to herself. More modestly, he . . . But the thought was a complicated one. And, though he was aware that it held a meaning that could be important, the requirements of his role didn't permit time for such probing.

Sometimes he would walk from the house along the drive between the rows of high, smooth, gray royal palms to the wrought-iron gates between white stone pillars. He would look out across the macadam road at the bleak inland expanse of low growing gray-green palmetto and the few spare stands of scrub pine, then note the wall of high, wide and luxuriant Australian pine across the front of the estate. The same sort of wall ran

111

along both sides of the place, extending to the sand of the beach. The trees on the outer edges were far enough away so that the wind, which stirred constantly through them, wasn't cut off from the house.

There were other trees within the enclosure—big tough banyans with cobra-like roots burrowing out across the lawns. There were beds of flowers within circles and squares and ovals of whitewashed brain coral. Poinsettia bushes and trees were in bloom on the north side of the house, which set midway between the front gate and the ocean. On the south side of the house was a small grove of four royal poinciana trees, now in vivid scarlet bloom all across the high rounded tops and sides. The house, a long, low, tile-roofed brown stucco built around a central patio, faced the ocean. Most of the roof was a vast mat of bougainvillea, in alternate strips of pink and red and purple. On the shallow slope of roof at the south end was a solar water-heating system, its glass panes glaring brilliantly, keeping the water almost constantly steaming hot.

The solar system impressed Ed more than anything else, and he'd return to marveling over it, shaking his head with the wonder of heating water without lighting gas or electricity. It was absolutely for free, and it was just close enough to a simple primitive miracle on one hand and the frontier of civilization and science and progress on the other to give Ed a feeling of awe and at the same time of well-being, of accomplishment.

On the third of the month a check came for Nora for twenty-five hundred dollars. He learned that such a check would come regularly and perpetually and he found himself spending considerable thought about it. Sometimes he had, in the past, played around with a stack of racing forms and figured how he could have, if he'd played them according to this system or that, starting in on maybe a capital of one or two thousand, managed to run up ten thousand. Then on a ten thousand capital, and getting the system down a little finer, he'd run up fifty thousand. It was easier to do with past results, of course, than trying with the results unknown.

He'd tried plenty of systems but he never got himself capitalized more than five hundred at any one time, and always, whether progression betting or long-shots only, or favorites to show, or double-ups, or the assiduous following of the consensus of experts, he'd find himself breaking the system. So when he would lose, he'd think it was because he hadn't had enough capital really to start right and play it comfortable. His living expenses would always interfere, too, and he realized that actually he could have made a steady income of the thing if only he'd not had to worry about the money.

But with twenty-five hundred a month regular, and playing, say on a thousand capitalization, he could make sure of playing the system through and cleaning up. Then gradually he'd increase his own capitalization, so that on the winnings he'd have plenty in a few months to play them bigger, and that way he'd have income enough so her trust-fund check wouldn't be needed at all. Of course, stocks were the thing, and he'd get in on them as a steady way of making a living, say by the first of next year.

Really big shots didn't get themselves tied down to offices. Maybe they kept an office to have some place to hang around for a change of scene, but once the dough was already there they didn't think like work-horses.

Then his mind would swing back to the fact and the actuality of the monthly check, and he'd figure out just how much that really was. Plenty. More than plenty. The reason for scrambling around for money was so you could have what he already had, and if you had it, you had it, and why think like a work-horse about piling up more? As a hobby, he could dope the horses. Or maybe buy out some ad outfits like 5-A, and let it just keep running as it was, with manager and salesmen doing the work.

These thoughts about the future, the adjustments of himself to a life of ease seemed important for a while. They troubled him because he was daily becoming more aware of a shift in his thinking. Whereas before he had thought of Nora and her money, now he was thinking of the money and then Nora. She was becoming the problem in his thoughts. He tried to make the problem go away by not thinking about it. But it was real. Gradually he found it would not go away. It was there. Twenty-four hours a day. He'd drive off for an hour or two, or sometimes more. He'd take a run back down to Miami Beach. Or he'd go up to Hollywood and make some horse bets and drop into a tavern for a while. He'd drive in to the nearest little town for groceries and he'd take the colored maid home at the end of the day's work. Or he'd just drive across to National Highway One and ride. Up as far as West Palm Beach. Down to Miami. Once he went inland along the Tamiami road that cut across the Everglades, but he'd come back. He wanted to go down the fancy road over the ocean to Key West, but it was a long trip. He wanted to go on a boat excursion, or charter a boat and get some swordfish or tarpon. But she wouldn't go anywhere. He couldn't budge her. After a few hours out alone he'd get uneasy and come home. Uneasy about something, he wasn't sure what—that she might kick him out? . . . no, he didn't think of it very often that way . . . that she'd do something?—what? Well . . . he didn't know. She spoke about forty or fifty words a day to him. She looked at him a lot.

Looked. Just looked. Not in any special way. Not loving or admiring, not angry. She never said anything to him unless he spoke. Sometimes she answered. Sometimes she just looked, then she would light a cigarette and look out at the ocean if they were in the house or patio. It would be evening or night when she was in the house. Days she was out on the sand in an awninged beach chair that faced the ocean. She would sit

114

there for hours. If he didn't come for her she wouldn't come in for lunch or dinner, he was sure. He would go out and say it was time to eat. He would say something about the weather or the water, or ask her if she was looking at the freighter which might be outlined, crawling past a few miles out. He would ask if she counted them . . . did the planes that came over bother her? She wouldn't answer. She would go inside with him, and eat. If it was still light after dinner she would go back to her chair. Sit. Look. Sit. Silent. He swam morning and evening. She might have watched him when he was in the water. She had nothing to say when he came to sit with her.

Just once he'd said: "Nora, there's something wrong. Nora, talk to me. Why are you so unhappy? . . . *are* you unhappy?"

She had looked at him, and there had been expression in her eyes and on her face and over her whole body that time. She hadn't said anything. Just looked, and he had thought it was hate. It had frightened him. He'd blabbed, demanded to know, talked, talked, got sore. She wouldn't open her mouth. He threatened to leave. She wouldn't speak. She looked away from him as if he didn't exist and stared at the ocean.

She slept in her own room and locked the door.

Of course she was artistic and temperamental and very unusual, but Ed had to believe it would all pass away. He didn't forget the way they had met, the sort of talking she had done there at the first. He didn't forget the episode with the elderly maid. She had been in a sanitarium, he remembered. But a man had only to look at her, to see how lovely, how normal and healthy she looked. All she needed was a little time. The fact that he loved her would bring her around and she'd be happy and herself again. Besides, women as a general rule were very moody and screwy when they felt like being.

Then, one night she began to talk.

CHAPTER II

FROM THE PATIO SHE COULD SEE THE moon rising—a massive orange ball. It rose, diminishing gradually, the length of her hand above the surface of the ocean; it climbed higher, stripping away its bulk and its color sifting down to vanish into the deepening layer of dark under it. It was higher above the ocean than the length of her forearm and hand together. It was compact, a small brilliant white circle, its rim sharply cut against the pale aluminum daylight of the night sky. She held her thumb and forefinger apart, holding it like a coin that has been worn smooth, a clean scoured perfect coin in her fingers.

And this coin moon had shaped and formed itself stripping away its superfluities bleeding out its colors, lifting itself out of the earth-bound density so swiftly. She had not breathed more than a few times, or blinked her eyes twice, before the great squashy ball had become this exquisite thing, risen and white, stripped of its impurities and of its heavy ponderous body. It had never happened before. The rising of the moon took hours, but now no more than a minute, surely. Obviously, time had undergone great acceleration. Still, there was no calculating it, for it was occasionally slowed to the point that hours would pass between the ticks of a clock. It was capricious to say the very least. It made her smile within—far back from the surfaces of her mouth and cheeks.

A capriciousness of the sort, she recalled, that she had had when she had been very young.

There was only one element that was constant and stable. The Gray Eyes.

116

They were with her.

Somehow, she was unable to maintain her will over her mind, though, and she found herself slipping back nightmarishly, time and again, time and again, to some weird but somehow terribly real hallucination. She would imagine that a man was with her. She would imagine that he talked to her and called her by name, and spoke endearingly; and most unsettling, he would seem actually to touch her.

One time his voice had come up out of the ocean, rising above the steady droning sound of it and becoming clear and articulate, and he had seemed to demand of her to be happy and to explain to him why she was not happy. He had persisted as real as—as her hands, as her feet—as real as her— He had persisted. He had not been just the droning, not just the distortions of sounds which sometimes made the waves seem like voices.

Like something rising from the ocean, a clear disembodied sound that might actually form itself. Distinct from the splashing, the spray, the dim faint roll of spent waves on hard-packed wet sand. Clear and different in every way.

The face had been so real, the touch so distinct, the tonal inflections, the facial expressions so detailed that he had been terrifying. She had concentrated, using every effort of will to dispel the terrible terrible hallucination. Visual. Auditory. Tactile. All of the aspects of every type of hallucination—except olfactory—no . . . not even excepting that, she had smelled the liquor and the mild odor of his sweat. Or had she, really? Such common odors, she might be filling them in in retrospect.

It was one thing to have had such hallucinations, the deeper implication of them was worse. Nora was aware that a part of her, a baser part, a successfully repulsed part of her desired a man. She could expect it as only natural that there might come fleeting wish-fulfillment fantasies of that sort, and she might temporarily imagine she DID have a man. But to have imagined him in such well defined detail was troubling.

Thin, rayon-cotton cocoa colored slacks. A loafer type of perforated brown leather shoe with buckles on the sides. A paler brown sport shirt with fly front so the buttons didn't show. Ornamental dark brown stitching around the cuffs of the short sleeves, the collar, the pair of big pockets. Dark hair, high wide, tanned forehead, lower face narrowing from broad cheekbones so his face had a sharp triangular look below the eyes which were—which were—some color—hazel, green, blue, black, brown? Hairy forearms, from above the elbows to the second joints of his fingers—wristwatch with expansible bracelet, commonplace enough. But once he had gestured, flinging his hand out to one side, and she'd seen a white scar clear across the palm. And how could she have imagined a detail of that sort unless, somewhere, in actuality in her remote past somewhere, someone . . . unless really there had been such a man—such a man, whom perhaps she had not known was important. Some man who had made a deep psychic impression in her. Unconscious.

Yes, it was damnably clear that that detail, that scar in particular, had really existed. It had been a part of some experience. A shock of some sort. Yes. And no. For he had cried out to her about happiness, as though really trying to bring happiness to her.

It was much too obscure. For some hours Nora thought about it while she smoked one cigarette after another. Much too complex and obscure. If ever there had been such a man crying out to her, wretchedly begging that she be happy, he was long dead. There was no point in thinking about it.

There was no point in thinking about anything. She had achieved communion with nature in its larger aspects. Her rhythm had at last become harmonized into the swift moon, was attuned to planetary space and motion. Unlike the swift moon, she was not a satellite of the greater and fuller rhythm of the Universe. She, like the swift moon, was attuned to planetary space and motion unlike the swift moon, she was not a satellite of earth. Neither was she dependent upon the sun. How trifling it was, how trifling the small bodies such as Earth, confined to endless petty grooves within finite space. Hurtling blindly and helplessly around its orbit unable to break free into uncharted paths . . . slave of its own weight and volition, entrapped by its physical actuality, at the mercy of a pinpoint of disintegrating energy called Sun; subject to perpetual enslavement, under the sun's own compulsion to self-destruction. It had become quite clear, and quite suddenly so, that Earth was, as matter always was, enslaved, and in a sense hypnotized into blind, deadly imitation of the Sun's self-destruction. So much that had never before been clear was so now. Imitation, the hallmark of man and ape, was simply a microcosmic instinct. Earth was itself the imitator of the Sun, man was of Earth's substance—Earth and man alike, perpetually and inflexibly, committed to eventual self-destruction.

The destroying and self-destroying Sun, which was but a pinpoint in space, was itself an imitation, the imitation of Destruction. Once Destruction had been called God Creator. Now it was clear that only because of Time did Earth continue to exist. Destruction, so vast that the blink of his eye was a hundred earth centuries, had sent his resistless will out into space, and set into motion the chaos and disintegration which appeared to Earth minds to be life because it was motion. What it amounted to was a great shuddering and trembling and vibration of such impact and intensity that the particles within Endless Space had been set revolting, tearing apart, burning out, disintegrating. Within the Earth's system it had been the Sun which was first to be destroyed; and its dying conflagration, its epitome of destruction was looked to and was depended on by the other planets, and worshiped by the creatures who saw it.

Nora had been most glad to leave the Earth, for to stay would have been suicide. Time, she hoped, was still her ally. Except for its capricious deceleration, it aided her in her escape toward the far end of Space to some haven centuries away from Destruction. It seemed to her that the God, Creator as he was once known but was now revealed as Destruction, was stationed at one end of Space, as at the end of a corridor. The Will of this great force had set into motion the various imitations and obediences to it from that one end of the corridor. Earth was somewhere about center of space. It was her notion that the Will of Destruction might not yet have penetrated the far end of the corridor, because of the delaying action of Time, and that she was in the process of going to this far end of Space where it would be motionless yet, and thus safe.

She would reach her destination over what appeared to be an endless ocean. Nora, though Ed had not realized it, had not once gone swimming, or so much as put a foot in the water. She hadn't done it even while they were in Miami Beach, though at that time, and before she had made love to him that one and only time, she didn't know why she avoided the water. She hadn't known then, in fact that the God Creator was Destruction, or that there was any haven for her at the end of Space. She had known she must hurry once more to a new and different world when she telephoned the real estate man. She had been in many worlds, but always before they had been earth-bound. There had not been quite so much urgency about leaving the unsafe one. She hadn't known that the world was in every part dangerous.

For a long time she had countered it with the belief that none of its inhabitants, and particularly human men, could ever, by any possible means, overpower her. Weak, completely. All bent before her. All were at her feet when she chose.

120

The old, the old women—they were the witches, the enemy, forever.

And she had to talk, sometimes. She discovered that. She had to talk. The Gray Eyes were constant. They were there. There. Always. Perhaps they had come for her from the other end of Space, but she did not know. They only commanded her to talk. Because? She didn't know. The Earth weight in her? Was it because this Earth weight, these heavinesses and pains in her impeded her journey? She believed so. There was no way to free herself, except to give the words to The Gray Eyes. They would carry the burden.

But she was afraid, too. Somehow. Why was it necessary to say the words?

Somehow, somehow—her head ached—somehow—it was as if—she didn't know—it was as if the words must be said aloud because they were motion. Yes. Sound was motion, of course; the waves of the ocean showed it. Motion was Destruction. At the other end of Space where Destruction's Will had not reached, there was no vibration and trembling and shuddering yet. And she could not be allowed to carry any such thing to the motionless end of Space. Perhaps that was the motive. Perhaps there was a danger that the sound-motion in her would set up sympathetic, imitative motion there in the motionless end of Space, and cause Destruction. Motion-sound—words words words of lie of hypocrisy of lies of broken promises of the weak . . .

The old women had stolen from Time.

Time.

Time. Stolen it. Time, the only protection from the Destruction stolen by the old women . . . stolen, and used and used to command the weak men . . . And the very young, who had not stolen Time were not able to take from the strong old women who must die.

". . . and then I took off the belt of my robe and made a noose, and the old woman slept and she did not know

121

I was there and I was going to put it about her neck and I would have killed her . . ."

"Nora . . . Nora . . . what are you saying? I know you had a fight with her, but . . ."

". . . and then I was afraid of her again because . . . I was weak. Why didn't I kill her? Do you think I was weak?"

"Darling, you frighten me. Don't talk like that . . . I know you're imaginative, and to listen to you is wonderful . . . I mean there was never anybody like you, but let's not talk about . . ."

". . . No, I wasn't weak. No, I was strong. She had knelt to me, she had been my footservant and she was helpless and I was her master, it was she who was weak, not I!"

"You shouldn't have thought about killing her. That was naughty. You hear, Nora. I'm scolding you, Nora. But I forgive you," Ed said. That was his role. To listen, to scold, to forgive. And— "Darling, darling, remember the rest of our game . . . remember . . . I always see you naked and beautiful and pure—remember? And I worship and serve and love you . . . wasn't that it?"

He was in front of her chair, and he crouched down, sitting on his heels, and looked at her and laughed. "So beautiful and pure and white . . . and wonderful, sweetheart . . . baby . . . baby . . . look at me, Nora, Nora . . . Nora, I love you!"

He remained. He watched her. She looked at him. She stopped talking and looked at him and she blinked her eyes and then she looked past him out toward the ocean. He lifted his hand and started to put it falteringly on her face. He wanted to touch her, to pet her. She had talked and talked. A dull terrible faraway voice. She had talked terrible gibberish . . . about an old woman and her father and a dog and a sailor and she said she was a virgin, she said she was pure. She would ramble off about a man who had gone on his knees and kissed her hands and begged her and she had made him leave his wife and she was pure and Adam had not and she

122

was a virgin and the bed was bloody and she screamed and his face was purple and his tongue had been out and swollen and thumb marks deep purple and there was the smell, and he didn't get fired, and then about trying to kill the maid . . .

She saw his palm as Ed extended his hand and she recoiled and screamed and lay back against the chair and stared out of glazed sightless eyes, rigid, rigid.

"Nora!"

She sat there, sightless, wide-eyed, rigid. Her fists were clenched. One hand held a cigarette, and the ember of it pressed against her slacks and the cloth began to smolder and he grabbed at her hand and tried to pull the cigarette away. He couldn't budge her hand. It was locked. He had to pinch off the burning end of the cigarette. It burnt his hand and the scalding sensation raced through his body and he sprang to his feet, and stared down at the hole in her slacks, and he knew her leg had been burnt but she didn't budge. She sat like stone. He watched her. He didn't move. The breath came tremblingly in and out of his throat and his chest burned and he was afraid, damnably afraid.

"Nora!"

She didn't answer. She didn't hear. He couldn't stand it. He walked across the patio, up the single step into the hall, off which led a lounge, a dining room and a kitchen. He went to the refrigerator and opened it. He slammed it and walked back into the patio. He stood looking at her rigid profile. She didn't blink.

He walked to her, walked past her line of vision, turning his head to watch her over his shoulder. She didn't give any sign of life. The irises of her purple eyes were fixed as though the eyeballs were locked from behind. The pupils were wide, black. Then, they suddenly contracted, but her eyeballs didn't move; there wasn't a flicker or expression on her face. He thought she wasn't breathing. But she was. Slowly, shallowly. The delicate flanges of her nostrils moved, indenting imperceptibly,

123

like a faint line accenting the lower roundnesses. Her pupils widened again and he bent near, almost touching her face, his eyes watching her lenses open into the black cavity. He peered there, holding himself only inches in front of her, trying to send his image through the dark channels that led back from the centers of her cornea, back into her consciousness. She saw him, she couldn't help seeing him.

"Nora," he whispered. "Nora, please."

He shook his head slowly in front of the wide open pupils, trying to force some recognition, even if only a movement of the eyes in their sockets. He stood back and lighted a match and held it near her face, then slowly moved it from side to side. The pupils contracted. That was all.

He walked out and stood in the middle of the kitchen, then he turned on water in the sink, and listened to the pump begin to chug. He took a glass, then changed his mind and shut off the water. He opened one of the cupboards and took out a couple of the two-ounce bottles of liquor with which he'd loaded a whole shelf. A rum. A gin. It didn't matter a damn. He broke the seal, unscrewed the cap of the gin and tipped it to his open mouth and drained it. He opened the other bottle and walked back to the patio.

She was lighting a cigarette. She glanced over at him, turning her head slowly, cigarette in her lips, and watched him over the flame. After awhile she whipped out the match, dropped it in an ash stand, still looking over at him. She took a deep drag of smoke and blew it out across her hand, and kept watching him, and her lips puckered thoughtfully, then relaxed, as though she had decided to speak and changed her mind. She let her glance slide down, then up at him again.

"Why did you try to burn me?" she said. "And slap me."

"I didn't, darling."

"Let me see your hand, I'll know. You raised it at me,

124

to strike me . . . didn't you? I'll know the hand well enough. Let me see."

"I wouldn't touch you . . . not to hurt," he said softly. He walked uncertainly toward her, holding the rum, unopened in his right hand.

"I'll know if it's true by the scar."

He slid a tube-steel chair across the tile, settled it aslant, sat facing her knee to knee. He leaned forward, elbows on his knees.

"Darling," he began softly. "Let's not play. Let's be serious. You know I didn't do anything like that. Nora, you were in a trance . . . I mean you were all stiff. Your whole body went stony, and you were holding a cigarette and it burned through your slacks, and I had to pry it away from you. Finally I had to break it off because I couldn't open your hands."

"I know you burnt me, whoever you are . . . you were here before and you were pretending you cared if I was happy, but you were lying of course, anyone who talks lies, and you burnt me and tried to force me . . ."

"Tried to pry your hands open . . ."

"Force me . . . and tried to hit me . . . burned my clothes, so that you could see me naked, that was it, I know, let me see your hand. I'll know if it was you."

"Look, darling, you're tired . . . upset . . ."

"Let me see your hand."

"You're insane," he said, whispering. "You are, aren't you? . . . It's true, isn't it?"

She looked past him, silent, began that same staring out at the ocean. Smoking. Ignoring him.

"I must never let the Sun see me again," she thought, "that has been the trouble."

Aloud, she said: "But I could have killed the old woman, I wasn't really afraid. I killed my husband and that proves I'm not weak and he was, you see. It proves it all. He was no world for me . . . I could have made it perfect but it wasn't worth it . . . unless it's worth while you don't bother making it perfect . . ."

125

"You didn't kill your husband, Nora. Don't talk like that."

"I killed him."

"Shut up . . . look at me and talk sense."

"I killed him."

"Nora!"

"I'm going to bed. Alone. Always remember that, you."

"Don't you know me, don't you really know me?"

"I don't know. Sometimes I think I do, and sometimes I don't know. But don't bother me. Please leave me alone. Please do."

"You think you'll get all right."

"Yes, it'll pass . . . oh, I'm so unhappy I want to die!" She ran into her room, closed and locked the door. There were tears on her cheeks and she began to laugh silently.

CHAPTER III

BY THE TIME THE SECOND MONTHLY check came their life together seemed hopeless to Ed. In his thoughts he sometimes emphasized the plural. Their life together was hopeless. He carried the check around, thinking about it, not mentioning its arrival. Sometimes she was lucid. Lucid enough to talk to him as Ed Harlon her husband, to ask him questions about such ordinary things as his trips in for groceries. Lucid enough to wonder aloud if she shouldn't return to Freelands.

One of those intervals might come at any time. The night before she had stood looking at the little calendar in the kitchen, looking at the five. It had been somewhere in the middle of the night between the fifth and sixth. She had torn off the five sheet, and carried it across to the container, lifted the top by the foot lever and dropped it in the pail. While she had the container lid open she lighted a cigarette and put the burnt match in the pail with a sort of strange, satisfied look on her face. She'd walked across to where he was sitting in the nook having some coffee, and he'd thought she would say:

"It's Tuesday, May 6. Saturday was the third. The check would have been mailed Thursday, and arrived Saturday. If it didn't arrive Saturday, which it might not have because there's only one delivery, it would still have come today, which is Monday—or it was until a while ago. Where is the check?"

She had that satisfied look when she settled onto the bench across the booth table from him. But she sat sidewise along the length of it, feet up, leaning against the wall, and smoked. When his cup clinked coming up and down from the saucer she glanced at him, and he was sure she was going to spring it at him about the check. But she didn't say anything. She was feeling satisfied and virtuous about not dropping the match carelessly somewhere, but putting it where refuse belonged.

So they didn't say anything. She smoked and the ashes spilled off and dropped partly on her blouse lapels, partly on her skin there below her throat. It was stifling hot and the ashes stuck in a dark patch, mingled with the sweat. He kept looking at the marring spot of dark there on her skin, wishing she'd wipe it away, but not wanting to mention it. He was thoroughly accustomed to her silences, but he preferred not to break into them any more.

He began to plan getting her signature on the check, but he was never sure when she might be lucid and he had to be careful. Not that he'd done a damned thing but he intended to, and he thought she might see he was feeling guilty about something. He didn't think she was playing any game, pretending to be bats, but she was unpredictable. When she would get to talking normally she went into the damnedest details, as though every trifle had been watched very carefully. A couple of times she told him just how many of the little liquor bottles

127

he had drunk in the past week. She told him the total number of bottles that had been on the shelf at the beginning of the week, how many replacements he'd brought in with the groceries Saturday, how much those combined totals amounted to, how many were left, and subtracted for him and named the amount that were left, which was what he had consumed, which averaged so much per day, etc. etc. If he cut himself shaving, or failed to take a shower, or had dirt on his clothes she would mention it and ask about it—not at the time, but two or three days afterward. Ask him interestedly, like a wife taking a check on things, without any reproof, but just to keep it clear that she knew what occurred.

She didn't seem to consciously try keeping check on everything. That wasn't it at all—at least she didn't do it aloud. She'd pick some one little thing out of a hundred, and go into and around and across and behind and over that one point—one point only—leaving out all the other ninety-nine. Just once in awhile she'd talk about herself, her condition. She'd leave him far behind, using terms he'd never heard, some of them.

". . . not paranoia because I don't think people are persecuting me, you see, and you see I have no scheme for changing the world and I don't think I'm anybody else but who I am, that is certain, why should I think I was Cleopatra or Salome or Joan of Arc or the Virgin Mary, why should I think I was anybody else? . . . And besides, there's a homosexual basis for it, and very definitely I'm not lez and I never had any desire to be, and I'm far from narcissistic, of course I'm no eye-sore and I know it and naturally I understand I'm pretty, but no element of self-love, you see; of course I have ups and downs, blue moods, gay moods, but that isn't a manic-depressive psychosis by any means, even if I soar happily I don't ever think of killing myself; and as for being schizophrenic, I'm not split-personality at all, because I am clearly what I am and simply because there are different aspects of my personality only shows I have a fair development

128

of interests; lots of times it's true I withdraw from the world, but we all have to do that sometimes, and if you are an individual at all, and especially if you have any creative talent you have to keep it and build it yourself and not let it be pushed around will-of-the-wisp by every trivial new idea that comes along, and you have to keep it inviolate from the destructive cross-pressures and not go about letting it be nibbled to pieces, and bent a hundred different ways to please a hundred different people; because if you are always yielding yourself, and reshaping yourself to fit yourself somewhere, the first thing you know you aren't anybody yourself, but a hundred little fragments of a hundred other personalities, and you are nothing but sugary mush for everybody else's taste and one day you look around and say where am I in all this, where did I go to, everybody just loves me because I have made myself out of parts of everybody else and that pleases them, but I don't find myself anywhere in the mess, and it's me I have to please first. I don't think people want to persecute me, you see, don't you, and that shows it's not paranoia . . . far from thinking they plot against me, I think they're incapable of any such boldness; men in particular are always plotting to offer themselves up to women, and not to overpower them. Maybe I should go back to my art, or my music, maybe I should go back to Freelands, maybe I am overlooking something. In my childhood there's nothing hidden; I know perfectly well all the loves and hates and shocks and disappointments I have had. I know all of these things, you see, and I don't think for a minute my mind is weaker than others, it's stronger, much stronger and it would be physical if there was really anything wrong with me, you see . . . something about the glands or nervous system or some physical aberration in the brain cells or failure of co-ordination between the lobes, some physical failure of the nervous tissue, and anyhow who knows about the mind—the brain, yes—but the mind! It is more than a machine for remembering

129

and controlling legs and eyes and seeing things that are
—I mean it is more than all of that—you see the mass
mind, the universal mind, that is to say, the big mind,
that mine is a part of, do you see? I mean the individual
brain is nothing but a part of the bigger one—not brain,
but mind, do you see . . ."

The talk would come to an end and in Nora's
thoughts she would try and correlate God Creator and
Destruction and find that as part of the All. Her mind
was subject to the same Destruction which caused the
planets to whirl to disintegration in Space, and the neces-
sity for getting to the far end of the corridor of Space
became more urgent, for it was never the flesh and body
but the mind which she needed to preserve, taking
it safely down to the other end of space to motionlessness
where the vast reverberations of Destruction had not yet
reached.

The part which more and more stayed in Ed's mind
when she talked about herself was the reference to Freelands. He didn't want her returning there, maybe to be
adjudged insane, maybe to find his marriage annulled.
He didn't want anything changed that way; he didn't
want to get in any tangle with the firm of attorneys who
handled her money affairs.

That night she sat smoking across from him in the
nook, and he kept staring at the ash smudge under her
throat. He wanted to ask for her endorsement on the
check. He wanted to deposit this one in his own account.
This one and the next and the next and next and—as
long as he could hang on—long enough to at least get
their marriage established. A few weeks was far from
enough to make his position strong. The attorneys would
make mincemeat out of his claims if she happened to
die, or if she got committed to an asylum legally. He'd
end up out in the cold without a cent. He wanted to
hang on, keep her sort of under cover, grab as much of
the money as he could. If she got well again and wanted
to get tough about it—well, as her husband, and with her

not mentally competent . . . That part he'd have to worry about later.

He took more coffee, and another smoke. She might go along, and she might not. If he asked for her endorsement and she got one of those clear streaks and began to take *him* apart . . . the way she could figure *herself* out . . .!

He walked out of the kitchen, across the patio into his own bedroom, got the check and a pen, and took them back and put them on the table.

"Endorse this," he said, putting the check face down in front of her, handing her the uncapped pen.

It was made out to Nora Emlaine, but that part was still all right.

"Endorse it," he repeated. His nerve started to trickle away on him. Damn! It was like living with an animal that you couldn't figure, that was figuring you all the time, and knew all it wanted to about you when it wanted to. Knew by instinct. She had plenty sharp instinct. She hibernated it, went around dull and stupid, then flashed it on you and showed you it was there sharp as hell . . . yeah, sure, she was shrewd. He got to thinking then . . . sure, it was all of it a goddam kind of game, after all. She said she was a killer and maybe she was; maybe he was prey in her own kind of manhunt. Not hibernating instinct, no, cat—cat, dozing—sure, now he remembered her drawing the lions; remembered how she thought they were wonderful superior creatures, beautiful, like she was—sure, dozing cat, but make the wrong move and she sticks out a paw and lays it on you and runs out the claws and punctures you a little.

Like her going along like a ghoul, then flashing out with professor talk about mental diseases, like she'd written the books and was going through the symptoms to test them out . . . like her knowing all the time exactly how goddam many ounces of liquor he drank, and then cutting out with it . . .

But she signed the back of the check. She paid no

131

more attention to it, but got out a new cigarette and chain-lighted it.

He was trembling when he screwed the cap back on the pen and scuffed the check with his finger so it slid across the table. He picked it up and blew on the ink, and read Nora—Nora Challis.

"Challis!"

"Yes?"

"Challis. Why did you sign it Nora Challis?"

"I never use my middle name. It's Gran's, too."

"You sign your name right—Nora Emlaine, sign it under this . . ."

"Of course if a thing is absolutely legal you would have to."

She took the pen again and wrote, "Nora Elizabeth Challis."

"That's fine!" he said with subdued fury. He broke out in a prickly sweat that needled the whole surface of his back from his belt up. Sharp swarming little points that itched and hurt at the same time. Sweat broke out on his head and rolled into his eyebrows. Goddam, the way she scrawled her names was terrible . . . the Nora Challis was on one line, but the second signature was bigger and she took three lines, and made the letters high, and it looked like the devil, and still the right one wasn't on it. "Under this, and in small letters and on one line, write Nora Emlaine."

"Must I print tiny? Tell me how to spell Emlaine."

He put the pen in her hand and said, "Don't print. Just write small. Write Nora, you can spell that—now write E-m-l-a-i-n-e."

He spelled it out, slowly, and she sat hunched over it, her face close to the table, her mass of reddish brown hair tumbled down, falling over her wrists, and sagging onto the table, and she nodded her head and said the letters with her lips after him, and moved the pen carefully. Every time she nodded, her hair would squash down around her wrist, and on the table. She held the

132

check with one hand and wrote with the other, and she'd laid the cigarette on the edge of the table, but he hadn't noticed. Then smoke began to crawl out of her hair, and he heard a little crackle. It couldn't burst into flame, he was sure of that, it would just crackle and smolder a little and die, and she was unaware of it, and he didn't want to stop her from finishing the signature. He said the letters, nervous, watching her nod and form the words and crawl the pen tediously over the paper; and the smoke continued to sift up through her hair there on one side and float, slow and lifeless upward, and he wasn't too sure it might not burst into flame. The needles of prickly heat were all over his back, and they began to stab in his scalp, and he could feel the sweat crawl tickling in the hair roots and before she was done the water was sliding down his neck and over his ears and coming off his forehead till his eyebrows were full to saturation. She finished.

She looked up and smiled at him and sat back while he reached for the check. Nearly half the back was covered with her writing. He wrote his own name quickly. He saw her look down and pick up the cigarette which had fallen on the seat beside her. He was wet all over. He wiped his forehead with the back of his hand, then ran a finger outward along each eyebrow. Some of the sweat ran stinging down into the corners of his eyes, and he knew his face was red and glistening. He wiped it on one sleeve, then the other, but the sleeve was soggy too. He looked down and saw his shirt was stained dark with sweat all across his stomach.

"I'm going for a shower," he said. She didn't pay any attention. She looked oily. She could use a shower, too, he thought, but he was glad to get away.

Under the spray he wondered how that check was going to go over at the bank. He wondered if she really had known damned well what she was doing, and if so how long before she'd come out with it—and then what . . .

CHAPTER IV

THE CHECK HAD BEEN ACCEPTED. Over a week now. No squawks on it yet from the point of origin. Well, screwy or not, her signature was on it. When her attorneys started going over their canceled checks at the end of the month though and saw those signatures and began to remember about her mind, and began to wonder about his name on there, and began to wonder—what? Wonder what! What could they do? Maybe come down and take a look, or maybe just get the machinery all ready to have her confined, and maybe come at him with some sort of fraud or conspiracy charge.

But she'd signed it to him, and it would be her word against his as to whether she authorized it into his account. But that wasn't the point . . . just her talk and actions and all of it would be enough to kill this marriage deal. Well, he was clear and in the velvet for a couple grand right now, and that was plenty. If he pulled out now he'd be smart. Or dumb. Sure, dumb. They'd have the cops on him . . .

He had had his fill . . . more than . . . more than. The day and night was turned around, as it was. She'd quit sleeping nights. He'd almost stopped it, too. Mostly he didn't sleep any regular time. Just napped an hour. Got out of the place in the car as much as he could, but he didn't stay away long. He was beginning to worry that the maid would begin spreading stories about the way things were. Not that she knew very much about Nora, but if talk got started and the authorities decided to look into things . . .

He didn't like to sleep while she was up and about, that was certain. He was afraid of her. He was repulsed by her, too—though he didn't like to think of that part.

But the plain fact of it was that she was dirty and messy now. And the plainer fact of it was—well, he couldn't stand even to think the words, but she smelled bad. She wouldn't wash or comb her hair or put on different clothes or take off the ones she was wearing asleep or awake. Her hair was in tangles and knots, and her face was oily and dirty, with dried goo in her eyelashes and in the corners of her eyes, and her lips were grayish pink, and crusty sometimes, and little rims of dirt at the corners, and it was worse than that even, but he didn't like to think about that at all. She'd look like a horror when she'd get out of bed somewhere around sundown, with her hair scraggly and stringy. She'd comb it away from her face with her fingers, and go into the bathroom. He'd got to listening outside the door, sick ashamed to do it, but doing it anyhow, just to check if she washed at all. She didn't. Not a whit. She'd come on out and eat the breakfast the girl had set out for her before leaving.

It was revolting. It was something he didn't know how to get at.

He came back from taking the maid down to the bus stop, drove back fast, knowing Nora was due to leave her room.

It was almost too hot to breathe. The heat lay like a hot mush poultice over everything, sucking what little energy and spirit there was left out of him. All he had was some raw nerves to keep him going. Sundown was the worst time of day, in some ways worse even than the blistering, murderous downpour of the midday sun. There was no air. Not any breeze. The waves kept rolling and rolling and rolling with a heavy sound like a sick wasp, and that sound added to the heavy airlessness. The damp, muggy hellish choking heat made him feel like he was going berserk.

He heard her stirring on her bed and he moved to the end of the patio, looked in the hallway entrance. She was walking around back of her closed door; he could hear.

He waited for her to unlock the door and come down the little hall to the bathroom. He was sure as hell going to say something about the way she looked—and smelled —God damn it!

He waited. He was stripped to shorts and sandals, but the sweat kept oozing out of him anyhow, though he was standing perfectly still. There were heat rashes all over him, and maybe the rashes were from more than heat. He'd swum a couple of days ago in water so tepid that he'd come out too exhausted to do anything but flop down when he got in the house. He'd got in a tangle of scummy stuff, seaweed, and sludge that had come washing ashore from out in the shipping lanes. He was getting so he hated the scummy water. The beach was nothing but a garbage catch-all.

She didn't come out. She was paddling around barefoot in there. The windows were closed all through the day in that room, and the door shut, and it was like an oven. He didn't see how she stood it. But she wouldn't open the windows before the sun was down. She had her reason, he was damned sure of that; but damned if he wanted to know what it was. She had her reason for not leaving the house, too, he was sure.

If he could only get in the car this minute and point its nose north and drive it straight through the night and get a thousand miles away from this hell hole. She was padding around, padding around in there. He wished she'd come out and get through in the bathroom so he could take another cold shower. Not that a shower did any good. There wasn't a dry towel in the place, because when they got wet in this humidity they stayed wet for days, and trying to dry your body was impossible. Rub away with a damp towel on the water, and before you were through the sweat was rolling down the furrow of your back. Put on the lightest shorts, and the pressure around your waist when you buttoned them made a red belt of prickly heat on your skin. Take a drink of whisky and it didn't even pause in your belly but began to hot needle your skin. Especially in this airless sundown hush he'd get to feeling that he was actually, honest-to-God suffocating. There just wasn't enough air mixed in with the water you breathed into your lungs, and if you tried to pull your chest full of air everything began to swirl before your eyes.

Out the land-side windows of the patio the sky in the West looked like one damned big choking bonfire, a big dead blaze buried in huge ugly layers of deep gray and purple. Sunk clear to the bottom of the sky bog, the last of the sun was a bloody glare. There was only a rind of it left and then it would be sunk and dead for good, he hoped. Land of sunshine! God, he could do with a glacier, a huge white mountain of ice floating in black ice water that you could dive into and stroke your way down deep with your mouth open and your eyes open and your arms and legs spread out, feeling the water icy cold and fresh and putting some life back into you.

He heard her windows open. The sun had sunk out of sight, though the sky was still light. Her lock turned and she came out.

She looked at him furtively, slipped warily past him, glanced back, ran into the bathroom, shut the door. He stood there in the patio entrance. She came out and she hadn't had time to wash. She came back to the patio entrance, looking down at the floor as she walked, not making any sound. She avoided looking at him, turned sideways, passed him. Her hair looked like it had been doused in thin grease, and stirred around in it till it was half congealed, then slapped into a stringy tangled tousle. She kept her head bent down and forward, and her shoulders sagged, and the dirty slacks and blouse were crumpled and wrinkled. Her feet were bare and dirty, the polish partly chipped off the nails. Sweat had run down drying and sticking, making dirty gray lines over her insteps. She scratched herself as she sluffed across the patio. He followed her to the kitchen, watched her sit down and throw back the cloth that covered cup

137

and saucer, glass, plate and silver. She went over and got out some milk and a half grapefruit. He waited for her to get settled with cereal and coffee at the table, then popped out some ice cubes. He put them in a big tumbler and poured water from one of the cold bottles in the refrigerator. He drank, slowly, letting the cubes lay against his lips. He drank another glassful, savoring it. It was good enough to make all his troubles fade. It came sweating out of him, but it wasn't the prickly, crawling hot sticky stuff, but like a cool flushing out. He could still feel the coldness in his mouth, and he felt a lot better. He thought there was a little breeze starting up.

"Wouldn't you like some water?" he said to her. She sat crouched over, eating, and didn't answer. Her nails were chewed down to the flesh, the polish chipped away to uneven rims at the cuticles. She didn't have on any rings.

"You need some water," he said. "Inside and out."

He took a glassful to the table. "Here, maybe you need some salt and water."

She looked at him, chewing with her mouth open, her face dirty and sweating. He unscrewed the top of the big salt shaker, filled half with rice to take up moisture, but the salt was thick and swollen with water anyhow. He spooned in for a quarter spoonful, flicking away the rice.

"Open your mouth and eat this," he said, extending the spoon. She did it. He held the water glass to her lips, and tipped it for her to drink. She kept swallowing without lifting her own hands till it was empty. Then she ate again. She was a mess, a plain mess.

"Maybe that salt will make you feel better," he said. "It's very important in a climate like this."

Sometimes it was like talking to a wall . . . most times. Or to a dumb animal. Or an infant. Except she didn't respond as much.

"The wind's coming up a little," he said. "It oughta be

138

cooler pretty soon. I don't think you should sleep closed in that room in this weather. That's not healthy, keeping your windows closed."

Her cigarettes were on the table, and he got one and lighted it. There hadn't been any breeze, Ed realized. He'd just thought it with the cold water and sweat giving him the sensation. There were supposed to have been electric fans, but the people here before them had carried them off, and the real estate guy was "seeing about it." If he could set one up and slant the airflow into the refrigerator and park there in front of the open door. The air hung dead. The smell from her seeped out through the room bad enough to gag him.

"Listen, Nora, what say we get cleaned up and go in to town? There's an air-cooled movie . . ."

She didn't answer. She was done eating. She started to smoke. Dirty and smelly and—and—forlorn . . .

"I guess you're tired out," he said. "It's this heat. Maybe you got a fever or something . . ."

He ought to take her to a doctor. But if he did that and she got to talking. . . .

But he either had to get away from her or do something for her . . . somehow. He couldn't sit around and watch her going to pieces this way. Lots of times when he would say: "Do this or do that" and go ahead with it for her, she would comply. Asking or suggesting was no good.

"Get up," he said, rising, going to her, taking her arm.

He took her out and across the patio to the bathroom. "Now, go on, and get in the tub and get yourself cleaned up."

It didn't work. It took words *and* action. He set the water running in the tub. She just stood there and smoked, finished a cigarette, threw it in the toilet and felt in her pocket, but the pack wasn't there.

"You smoke too much," he said. He unbuttoned and took off her blouse. Her brassiere was a series of wave-lines of dried dark sweat. He took it off her. Her breasts

139

and skin were all broken out. He got her slacks and panties off of her, left her standing while he gathered the stuff in a heap and carried it out. He went out of the house with it, clear to the incinerator down at the beach end of the row of Australian pine. He flung her clothes in it, gritting his teeth.

The water was sucking down the overflow when he got back. She stood precisely where she had been. He turned off the water, drained out about half of it. "Get in," he said, taking her by the elbow. "Step over . . . now the other foot . . . sit down . . . keep hold of my arm." He slipped an arm around her, helped her lower herself.

"Here," he said, giving her soap and a brush. "Go on . . . start in . . ."

She didn't do anything with the soap and brush. Just sat holding them.

He had to do it all for her. He was as wet as she was, part water, part sweat. On his knees in his shorts there on the tile beside the tub, he worked. It was a little funny. A guy could dream of a thing like this. Giving a dame a bath. But it wasn't like that at all.

He showered her, left her standing in cold spray while he probed around her room, getting underthings and a pair of sandals. He carried them in his own bedroom where it wasn't messed up so bad. He went back and looked through her dresses, decided finally on a sort of cool-looking lime and white cotton dress that buttoned down the front and had a little white belt.

A funny thing came over him after he got her dried and into the clothes. It had sort of started while he was working on her in the tub, because she'd not done anything for herself. He got to feeling very tender. It had been a long time since he'd felt sorry for anybody without at the same time having an unpleasant sensation along with it.

He looked her over, sitting quietly on his bed, clean and dressed. Her hair was still wet, but there wasn't much to be done. He got out some of his dry undershirts

140

and used them for towels and got her hair a little drier. He combed it and it took a long time to get some of the snarls out. Then he brushed it. It was dark out, and he snapped on the light. She sat there passive. He went back to her room and got her lipstick and brush. He pulled a chair up close in front of her and started to apply the lipstick brush.

Jeez, he felt like something. Maybe he was getting cracked too, but he sort of felt like he'd created her. He worked carefully, completely enrapt with the job of making her mouth pretty. Just like an artist. That's the way he felt.

He finished and got up and looked at her and said: "Now you're sweet again . . . like you were born to be." Jeez, he felt like something, he repeated to himself. He didn't remember ever feeling so good. He ached in his chest. She just sat there, and started to smile at him all of a sudden like she was saying he had made everything all right for her again.

He'd never felt like this. It was like he'd taken something that was thrown out and beat up and gone to hell and made it beautiful. It was like he'd really done something for her. Accomplishment . . . no, hell no, nothing like the feeling when he beat some sucker's ears off with a fast spiel and made him kick through with a big ad. No, not that kind of stuff.

It was like she was really his now, she depended on him and knew he was somebody and knew he loved her like he never had loved her—or anybody. Jeez, he ached with it.

"Look at me," he said. He laughed. His shorts were wet and dirty, and the rest of his body was a mess too. "Come on out in the patio, and I'll shower."

He went and got her by the arm and led her out, and sat her down and got her a cigarette and lighted it for her. Then he walked around the patio, not wanting to leave, thinking there must be something else he could do

141

for her. He went out and got her some ice water, then he set up a card table for her, brought out a deck.

"I'll be right back," he said. "Play cards or something. Then we'll have some two-hand solitaire or something. We'll have a swell evening . . . I'll make up some lemonade later. Gets cooler we'll have some of that sliced chicken . . . and Nell made the damnedest lime pie you ever seen. I'll be right back . . . you just enjoy yourself, baby . . ."

CHAPTER V

SHE BELIEVED THAT THE HOUSE WAS A space ship. She knew she was not alone in it, but she was unclear as to Ed's identity. She was trying to exist as nearly without thought or sensation as possible, but he had touched something when he sat before her, concentratedly painting her mouth. She had felt the movement of the brush against her lips, and had known that a nice thing was happening to her. She thought perhaps he was a doctor or her father.

But she could not be sure.

By now she knew she had enemies. Allies of the Sun, against which she closed herself off there in the room beside the ship's engines. One day she had peered out into the daylight and seen the man who had come with the power mower to cut the lawns. She had believed, seeing him near one of the banyans with its snaky, burrowing roots, that he was fastening the big cables into the Earth to keep the space ship grounded.

Much of the day when Ed thought she was sleeping, she lay sweltering, awake and feeling a sort of indefinable terror. She knew that she was on Earth, and that daylight always found the space ship stopped, and on Earth things could happen to her. Something . . . something terrible.

She had managed for years to disguise to herself her basic belief that she was somehow being pursued, persecuted, plotted against. As in many other things, Nora had twisted it around to the belief that other people were too weak to pursue or persecute, that they were the ones being pursued by her, and made to yield to her when she was in contact with them. Since her teens she had understood that the fear of plots against oneself denoted something dangerous mentally . . . so she had managed to reverse it.

In finishing school, and in college she had read extensively, almost obsessively of abnormal psychology, psychiatry, case histories by the score. In her case it resulted in a great deal of knowledge which she used as a shield, and to guard against standard, recognizable symptoms. It was a matter of self-preservation. She succeeded in avoiding obvious categories. She might have succeeded in understanding if she had been able to really trust anyone or anything. As it was, it had simply amounted to delaying action.

In everything she did she sought originality; and what she had once done she didn't want again. If she had been able, she would have changed homes repeatedly; she would (and she had) changed continually her set of friends—changed, in fact, whatever world she was in for another . . . for a better, it seemed to her, world . . . for a more advanced one. Always she had to feel she had advanced. She would go into a new world—whether it was the world of music or painting or of Freelands, or of new people—and remain until she believed she understood and had mastered it.

Eventually the progression would come to where it had. The feeling of having launched out into space, leaving the Earth entirely. The matter of Time, which she had thought about in varying degrees of the fantastic for years, was correlated to space in a close enough relationship to scientific fact to satisfy her. To progress, to go ahead from one point to another, into new environments, into new viewpoints was to keep abreast not of the times but of Time itself, to Nora. It was compulsive. It accounted for most of her vagaries, her dissatisfactions, her carelessness . . . she was always under some compulsion to keep going, not to be delayed, to get on, away, forward in space and Time.

Sometime she would arrive at the point, she knew, where she would achieve a safe place to stop. A curious ambivalence. She had only recently become aware that it had always been her ambition to stand still . . . that her whole teen age and adult life with its abnormal sense of continual racing with Time was based on the opposite desire. A few years ago she would have recognized an underlying death-wish against herself in it. She would not have been able to recognize that her forward flight was the opposite of the deeper need—to go back. To somehow leap terrible obstacles and arrive at a point in *past* time . . . a point in the third year of her life. Before that point there had been little fear or unhappiness. Beyond it—too many things set too deep and menacing for her ever to know again.

Now she was cut off, split apart. She struggled unconsciously to leap those years, to be a child. But it was an almost hopeless struggle, and she knew it . . . not in any articulate knowledge, but in the encompassing sense of fear and helplessness. She believed there was another woman in the space ship who was not to be trusted, and who conspired. This woman was herself . . . the self which would sometimes sit and discuss the mental troubles of Nora. Who would sit and talk to the man and talk of long detailed Earth matters, *trying to bind her with those details, as though such earthly matters were ropes that were holding her and the space ship to Earth.*

It was true. The occasional launching out with words, with carefully detailed observations of small matters; the discussion of paranoia, of schizophrenia were all efforts of a part of Nora to hold to, to prove that she had a grasp on, reality. But it was a constantly diminishing part of her, a slowly evaporating and weak element. After the effort she would be abnormally listless and depressed, and the slow cloud of fright would settle over her again. The fright was not long endurable, and then her greatest flights into the fantastic would come.

The role of the lucid Nora would be gone over, as she lay closed in, sweating, in the blinded stifling heat. The other Nora was clever, cleverer and much older than she, and she worked with the man, and signed statements against her; and she did not know what the statements were about. She didn't know exactly what purpose the woman had in informing on her. Whether the man was a detective or a psychiatrist she didn't know. But she knew that it was some sort of effort to trap her, and either jail or confine her in an asylum.

The Gray Eyes were a curious element at this time. She was certain that they really had a face, and that all of the years The Eyes had watched her they had really had a face which they dared not show her. She was not sure whose face . . . but someone's, and this someone was an enemy but he was a friend. She knew that it was so. It made no sense to her, but it was so. Both friend and enemy.

At any rate, she was careful of what she let The Gray Eyes know now. The other Nora, the one who conspired to trap her on Earth, looked like her, and she did not know if that might account for The Gray Eyes being friend and enemy too. Friend to one of them, enemy of the other . . . but which was which?

The Gray Eyes were both man and woman, too!

He saw it was hopeless after an hour. He sat across the card table from her, and she made gestures at playing double solitaire after he dealt for her. She watched him and put down cards from her deck when he did,

145

and scanned her deal the way he did. When he turned up an ace and put it out in the middle, she picked up an eight and put it on his ace. He started to say something about it, but changed his mind, and tried to play his own game. She watched him and turned a card when he did, and seemed content just to ape his movements.

He couldn't take it. The hell of it was she seemed to be trying to please him by doing what he did. It was different and better in a way than when she didn't know he was there. But he'd look at her and think she was sweeter than anything he'd ever seen, and realize she had less understanding than an animal. Not a plotting, wary one.

He thought he'd rather have it the other way. He didn't know . . . he didn't know . . .

He tried to talk. She nodded if he did, and mirrored his smile, and then it would fall dead. She didn't pick up the conversation. If he went blank, quiet, so did she. She hung on him with her eyes. She followed him to the kitchen, waited for him to say or do something. It was as if she loved and trusted him . . . the way of a dog— not even that though, because a dog would have had some antics of its own.

He turned on the radio, and kept faced away from her. He gave her a smoke. He really felt sick. Jeez, since he took charge of her and bathed her and prettied her up it was as if he'd bought her, and he was God.

He tried the card table again, distracted himself at any rate, and kept glancing at her, saw she was doing just as before. He grinned at her. She returned it. What was she thinking? Anything?

He got a little kick out of it, too, in a way. It was flattering.

After awhile she dozed off in the chair. He was relieved. He didn't bother her. He walked back and forth, trying to figure how the hell to think about it. If she continued in this kind of a relationship to him, he'd be able to stand it . . . maybe. He'd be able to do what he wanted with her. But she was the same as dead, and it wasn't right. She had to have a doc. Then? Then maybe he wouldn't have her at all. Nor the monthly checks either. No, that wasn't it, that wasn't it . . . honest to God not, he told himself.

Besides, how long would this role of hers last? Sure, she was easy to handle and sweet as a baby—now. But how about the kind of temper she'd had that night with the old woman maid? What about in the shower in the Miami Beach hotel when she'd smacked out at him? How about the time she gave him that devil of a look out there in the beach chair?

After all, the way she had kept repeating that night that she had killed her husband! Couldn't forget it. No matter if it was the truth or not, if she *thought* like that she might just take a notion to really kill somebody—him. He wondered if he was still Gray Eyes. Or if he was Gray Eyes again . . . or how the hell he stood. If she took it in her head to think he was slapping her around and burning her clothes off of her the way she had once, she might do anything.

He decided to make a stab at something when she woke up. He brought his chair near and started in cautiously.

"What about that place—that Freelands you were at? They treat you pretty good there, baby?"

She cleared her throat. She pushed back impatiently at her hair. She looked at him, and blinked, puzzled. He cursed himself. Damn, he shouldn't have broken the spell!

"All I mean is, I'd like to hear about it . . . nothing important about it . . . just interested."

"I've been there . . . that's behind."

"Sure it is. I know that. Far behind. Don't even think about it. Forget I asked," he said. "Come on, let's have something to eat. Come on . . ."

She wasn't so pliant, and she dragged at first, but she went with him.

147

After they ate she dozed in her chair again. She woke with a sharp cry and looked around her, her eyes wide and frightened. He moved over to her, took her hand.

"What's wrong, Nora? Don't be afraid. It was just a bad dream. I'm here . . . don't be afraid . . ."

She sat staring, breathing hard. She let her hand stay in his. She looked slowly from one end of the patio to the other, then stared out toward the ocean, her eyes cloudy. He patted her hand. She turned her face to his.

"Ed," she whispered. "Ed . . . say it's you . . ."

"Ed, yes. I'm Ed. You do know me, don't you, darling? I love you. I don't want you to be afraid."

"Please do something. Listen fast . . . listen, Ed. I can't stand it any more. Listen fast to me talk, because I don't know what goes on any more: . . . Tell me where we are. . . . We're in Florida, on the shore, aren't we?"

"Yes, darling. Listen, Nora. You've got it all right, all of it. You can pull out of it, can't you, if I help you, if we get a good doc? . . . All you need's help . . ."

"No. No. Ed. Listen fast, because I can't help myself . . . I really can't, honest to God I can't, believe me. Take me away, now . . . take me to the police . . . aren't we near Ft. Lauderdale? Take me there, and wire New York police . . . no, they'll do that in Lauderdale. . . . We came in there . . . that's where we put in from the cruise to Cuba . . . my father and his girl and the dead boy. No, I'm tired, I'm the one. Adam was his name. I was twelve . . . listen, Ed . . . I mustn't be alone with you . . . never. Things happen . . . too much. I did kill my husband. . . . I really did, Ed . . . this is cold sober truth . . . and I don't know why I killed him. Another woman . . . he took me back, but then he was revolted with me, Ed, and I did it . . . I did it . . . I can't stand it . . . you must turn me in. . . . I remember Adam's face, Ed, it was bloated, and there were purple blotches on his throat . . . tongue was thick and out, and we put in at Lauderdale. That part doesn't matter, but I can't stay here. I'm afraid, Ed, I tell you. . . . Ed, the sound of those waves, they drive me cr—they drive me nervous. I think of them like they were out in somewhere . . . out in some place in the sky . . ."

". . . Nora, your husband killed himself, you told me that when you were yourself, Nora. Don't you see you couldn't have got by with killing him, you couldn't have hanged him, not a little woman like you. How could you have done it? If you hit him, the police would see the bruises. He'd have had to be unconscious for *you* to have hanged him. And you couldn't have handled him anyhow . . . not without the police seeing it wasn't suicide."

"But I did, I tell you—I did . . ."

"You imagined. You got your mind all upset with grieving over him and imagined it . . . but now you've got to stop that stuff. He's gone, darling, he'll never come back. You must forget him . . . it wasn't your fault. Don't you love me any, not any at all . . . don't you? Can't you forget him?"

"No. But it isn't love that makes me remember. I swear to God, Ed. . . . No, you don't understand . . . I'll telephone the police myself."

"And leave me? You don't give a Goddam for *me*, do you? Not a bit of it. I tell you you're upset . . . I tell you you have been ever since we met. You started right in with that idea that you had to confess to somebody . . . to me . . . to me instead of the police."

"I'll tell you in detail, Ed, just how I did it."

"No. Tell it to the police. If you've got to go . . . let them take you . . . they'll come . . ."

"Ed, I know you feel terrible about it, because it's hit your whole life and you think you love me, but you don't much."

"I do!"

"I like your saying that, but—"

"Nora! What if you DID kill him? It's done. Can you bring him to life by going to jail?"

"Give me a cigarette . . . it isn't jail for me I'm afraid of . . . I don't want to go on like this . . . I don't know what I might do. I might kill somebody again . . . YOU, Ed. I mean it. . . . That's what woke me up from that nap. I dreamed you were hanging Ed . . . now do you understand?"

"Yes."

"Then make me get out."

"No . . . I can't."

"Do you think I'm sane?"

He didn't answer.

"You see?" she snapped. She got up from the chair. "I DO think you're sane. Listen to you. Do you know what's going on or not?"

"Sure I do. Absolutely. What I'm trying to say is something you don't understand. It comes over me. I can't control my mind. That's all."

"You're controlling it now."

"Sure I am."

"You can keep on if you want to."

"I do want to."

"I think it's nothing but grief."

"You really think so?" Nora said.

"Absolutely. You were married for years and you must have loved him . . . not that I like the idea, but you must've. When he went it knocked you for a loop."

"Don't you remember I was in an asylum BEFORE that?"

"Would they have let you out if you weren't OK?"

She laughed. "I was too smart for them. That's all."

"Oh, sure. That's what you think."

"That *is* what I think, Ed. There's something else I think. I think I'm sane now, and I think I'm going to stay that way."

"That's better."

"They say 'Once a schizophrenic, always a schizophrenic,'" she said, walking agitatedly back and forth. "That's what some of them say. It's not so, though. Is it?"

"Well, if that's what you were, it's not so."

"Schizo means split personality," she said.

150

"Yeh, I remember."

"Like you're two different people. Opposite people," she said. "I never was schizo anyhow. Not really. For instance, Ed, I'll prove it. I wouldn't ever let myself think I was really a murderess if I was a schizo—or almost any type psychotic—I'd not accept that fact. But I do. I am a murderess."

"You insist on that."

"I have to. If I start denying a fact like that I'm insane for sure. I couldn't forget it," she said. "Now, don't you see?"

"I guess."

"It's up to you, Ed. Can you take me, knowing this truth?"

He nodded. He didn't know anything else to do.

"A really insane person thinks the rest of the world's crazy," she said, laughing. "Not him. Oh, no. Never will you find him admitting it. But you see, Ed . . . I didn't claim I was sane . . ."

He remembered she had though.

"The funny thing is about paranoiacs. It's a wonderful type of psychosis. Simply wonderful because that type can sometimes go along all their lives without ever being suspected. Because they are brilliant, you understand. Brilliant. Strong, superior minds. With a command of logic that makes a fool out of the average smart person. They can create whole new systems of philosophy, whole new worlds, vast new systems of religion. Some of the most famous saints and philosophers were paranoiacs. They have been the master-mind murderers, the ones who took pride in it as a work of art . . ."

She glowed, he saw. Exhilarated. As if paranoiacs were her supreme heroes.

"These people often have brilliant careers in every business and profession. They are respected and admired, socially and intellectually . . . and all the time underneath it they are insane . . . and they kill . . . and they're not caught. Sometimes they are, but—" she broke off to

151

extinguish her cigarette. She put a fresh one in her mouth, lighted it, paced again, scanning him with a flushed face, bright eyes as she passed. "Often they delight in planting clues that lead to themselves. They set the wheels of justice to work at their own pleasure if they need punishment . . . otherwise, no . . . they're not caught. For instance I would confess to someone, and they would think, ah, now they have me, now they have a grip on me—but I would simply say: 'Prove it.' People go about looking for screaming, shrieking maniacs; they think that's how to know insane people . . . ah, but that's not so with para—"

"Look, will you shut off this wild talk?"

"What's the matter . . . what's the matter? Don't you like to hear about madmen?"

"Not so loud, I don't . . . jeez you been practically screaming."

"Oh . . . have I? I didn't know—but of course I knew . . . I feel good, that's all. I FEEL like shouting . . . I know I'm not insane, isn't that something to shout about?" she cried. "Isn't it now? Of course."

"I feel personally like a drink."

"I'll join you . . . yes, indeed, Ed, most of the world never had the brains to go off the track in the first place. It takes more brain voltage than they've got . . . that's all . . . just the herd, that's what people are . . . weak, corrupt . . . they yield and knuckle under or sell out . . . it's all the same . . ."

"Let's talk about something else," he said opening the refrigerator.

"Uncomfortable, Ed? Afraid of something? Most people are. And why not? . . . keep them in line, in their place . . ."

"Did you really kill the guy?"

"Can you prove it?"

"I just asked you."

Nora laughed. She closed her eyes. "My God, my head

152

aches, my God, it aches . . . I'm so tired, so damned tired . . ."

"Weather," he said.

"Weather . . . weather, weather . . . is THAT what you'd rather talk about? Such brilliance . . . let's talk about the weather, oh, let's do!"

"Do you want a drink or not?"

"No, I don't. Swill yourself as usual."

"God damn it, I need it around you."

"Ed, don't argue with me . . . please don't . . . didn't I tell you what to do, didn't I, Ed? Didn't I try to tell you to get me out . . . take me out, to make me, to make me go, oh, for God's sake, I'm tired . . ."

"Go lie down awhile."

"I'm going."

CHAPTER VI

IT WAS ALMOST THREE IN THE MORNing. Ed stood in the open doorway of her bedroom, staring into the dark, listening to her whimper in her sleep, seeing her writhe sometimes and lurch. She had been tossing about for a quarter of an hour. He'd snapped on the light once but she was locked in sleep. He took a long drink from the highball in his hand, watched her and shuddered.

In her dream she was laughing, but she was in terror, complete terror and the sounds of her laughter were raucous-throated squalls. She was laughing and playing naked on a bed, and a man was there naked and she was squirming because he had his hands on her naked bottom and tickling the opening there at the bottom of her stomach, and he was naked too, and on his back and what was at the bottom of his stomach that she was giggling and playing with while he was tickling was a

153

funny dog that would get up when she coaxed . . . and she was giggling and giggling and having fun and Gran ran in and she yelled and she picked up a chair and she tried to hit them and Nora crawled under the bed and she could see Gran's feet and hear the yells and the things breaking, and after awhile there was some blood out on the rug and the man was crying only it was in her throat, that crying, raucous-throated terrible terrible squalling in her throat while she was giggling in the dream. And after that Daddy didn't live there and he didn't play with her and make her giggle and she wasn't happy and it was because of Gran who was old and ugly and mean and would not let him live with her, and when he would come to visit Gran would tell all the bad and wicked things, and in the dream she went in the big room and Gran looked out at her from the dark and didn't know she was there under the tall arched windows with a box to kill Gran, and Gran called out because she was afraid of her she was so mean, she was the meanest girl in the world, she would always be meaner than every other girl, she told Gran, and she was riding suddenly in the dream and a woman was saying ". . . in the islands girls of that age are already doing it, doing it doing it all the day long." "I forbid . . ." Daddy stood high and said to the woman "I forbid" and Adam came and laughed and laughed and said "You are some sailor, what kind of a sailor are you? . . ." "But I am a virgin, I am twelve, and it was Adam, yes he was the one who came in the cabin, and it was night and the woman said the girls do it on the island, and the door opened and that is who it was, and that is why he is dead, because of that, because Daddy forbid him to rape me, and the bed was bloody."

She laughed and she laughed. And there was a sick feeling from the swaying in her stomach and the door opened and the man was breathing loud, and he came across the room, and he stood by the bunk and she looked up at him in the dark, and then she tried to yell and a big hand went over her mouth and she bit into it, but it was happening and it was happening and it was happening and the ship is rocking all the day long with girls of that age in the islands in the islands and a man had come running along the deck while it was happening and he ran in and there was a fight and a fight, and Adam's throat was purple from the thumb mark and we will go to Ft. Lauderdale, because he tried to rape my daughter, yes sir, yes sir, we understand, and Adam smelled and he swelled up and it is a justifiable homicide and whose pretty little girl are you and how lovely a child of twelve is daddy's girl and Gran is mean, and there are teeth-prints in Daddy's hand, he never shows his hand, but I know and I know and I know that there are teeth-prints in his palm, because I know and because I know and it wasn't Adam but it was justifiable it was justifiable and the gray moon face was watching her and it came down from the sky and did not rise and it came down and it stood at the window and it watched and it had gray hair and then gray eyes and it was coming slowly into the room, and it said: "I am Gray Eyes." "No, you are Gran." "I am Gray Eyes." "No, you are Gran, and you are Daddy." "I am." "Go away." "I will never go." "I killed you, Gran, I killed you with the belt of my robe . . ." "No, you don't hate me." "But I do, I do . . . It's you I hate, do you hear that, Gran? . . ." "No. You know that you can't hate me." And the moon darted up to the ceiling and she twisted around, hid from it. "You don't hate me . . . you couldn't kill me." "Go away. Listen to me laugh because I hate you." She laughed and she laughed. She laughed. The huge face hovered, closer and closer and then whispered. "You are crying." "I laugh." "You are crying. You know it is I who have been with you. I who saw you clean and white and naked and beautiful . . . my eyes always. . . . It is my gray hair that is my eyes and WE KNOW." No. No. No. "We know . . . the shame of it . . . the shame of it . . . a child of

155

three . . . my son . . . we know . . . we know, Nora Elizabeth Challis." "Don't call me that, please."

And then it was all black. She sat up in bed, still asleep, still in the dream. She whispered, "Gran, if I whisper it to you will you come back and see what I am? . . . Gran, will you be sorry when I die? . . . Gran, you know I am good . . ." There was only the black. There were no windows, just the blackness. Something moved back of her, something moved below . . . she was rocking from side to side . . . a sound of waves lapping, whispering. She ran out of the cabin and stood at the rail, listening to the whispering. "Gran, is that you, whispering . . ." "You killed the wrong one, it wasn't him at all, it was only Mr. Emlaine . . ." She strained forward, bending closer and closer to the whisper, and her hair caught on the top of a wave and she dove in but it was not water . . . just space . . . she kept falling . . . down . . . she spread her arms and banked off to one side, then looped, then dove down deeper and deeper when suddenly there was a man hanging and he said politely, "I forbid that sort of talk . . . it is not the sort of talk of a lady. There are exactly twelve teeth marks, you may count them for yourself: the upper canines, the incisors, remarkable for a bloody cat of 12 to have 12 teeth. . . . Now, if you will tighten my noose I will play the tickle game with the little hole at the bottom of your stomach. . . ." She began to giggle.

Ed ran to the bed as she screamed. He shook her. "Wake up . . . my God, how you screamed."

She clung to him, trembling violently, her fingers digging deep into his shoulders, and she breathed hard and fast and cried hoarsely. Her face flooded with tears and she pressed it hot against his shirt and held with her digging fingers, and then she let one hand free and slid in down his shirt, down across his shorts.

He kissed her. She put both arms around him. He lay down beside her, and she rolled over into his arms. He petted her and she put her mouth up to be kissed again.

The room was swaying slightly from side to side, she could feel the motion in her stomach.

He began to make love to her. She did not protest.

Suddenly he leaped off the bed with a roar of horror and outrage. He ran from the room. He flung into the bathroom, stepped into the tub—shoes, shorts and shirt on. He turned on the shower and moaned and began to unbutton his shorts. She had evacuated bowels and bladder . . .

Nora lay motionless swaying in her bunk as the ship rolled, listening to the waves. They were alone. If he ever got the ship to Lauderdale it would be too late. She had to kill him.

The bunk was still wet with her blood and she was weak and sore inside from what he had done and she got up, slowly, and sat for a moment adjusting to the rocking of the boat, and getting her breath. She pulled up the end of the sheet and dried the blood from herself and walked carefully around dead Adam on the floor and went to find him and get him before he could tell them lies.

She had to get some rope first, and she went to the galley, but of course there would be no rope there, but a knife would do as well, and she came back with it and waited for him to finish his shower and come out . . . and he didn't come out at all, he just stayed in there trying to hide.

She opened the door, and turned out the light, and he yelled: "Nora!" And she leaped and held the long knife in both hands and he flung up his arm and when she struck out with it, the blade glanced his arm and then buried in his side just under the ribs. He fell into the tub, loud, very loud and he kept yelling. She pulled the knife out again, and jumped into the tub with him, and he raised himself up and flung her back hard against the wall, and she could see the blood gushing dark out

of him in the dim light, and the water from the shower
was vibrating against her back and as he hurled her
away the water ran on her head and he was on his knees
and he was crying loud, and holding his side, and he got
to his feet and stepped over the tub edge, turning sideways just enough so that his stomach was in her direction and she swung out with the knife and it buried and
he fell out onto the floor over the tub, taking the knife
with him. She stood under the shower watching his dim
figure writhing and she heard the knife clatter against
the other wall as he got it free, but he couldn't get up,
and all of his blood was coming out on the floor. And
after awhile he just lay there, not moaning and not
moving and she went out to get some rope and hang him
so the police in Lauderdale would know it was suicide,
and she would tell them the whole reason for it . . .
how he was going to say it was Adam, and when she
really knew who it was because of the teeth marks. The
Gray Eyes said, "Well at last you admit what he really
was . . ."

Nora nodded. "Yes . . . but now I must find a rope."

She searched and searched and there wasn't any rope
and the ship was coming nearer and nearer Lauderdale
and she had to hang him so that everything would be all
right . . . but there wasn't any rope.

"Not in their world," said The Gray Eyes.

She turned out all the lights and then she could see,
and there was a rope, she made it with her mind, and
then she took it in and hanged him, and it was no strain
at all because she didn't have to use her body at all, just
her mind, and then she went back into her cabin and
crawled into her bunk and lay in a tight curl on her side,
her arms hugging her legs up against her chest, her
head against her clamped-together knees, and she could
feel the sweet, gentle swaying of the ship, and then the
ship was sinking and she could feel the sea warm around
her and there were no sounds anywhere and no light,

158

and it was beautiful there and she was clean, clean, clean, but it was strange and she cried a little, silently, because there was no one to hear, there was no one to see her, no one to care, no one who knew. There was no one, anywhere.

"I am here," said The Gray Eyes.

www.ingramcontent.com/pod-product-compliance
Lightning Source LLC
Chambersburg PA
CBHW022131170626
46808CB00002B/951